HELEN HALSEY

The Simms Series

JOHN CALDWELL GUILDS
General Editor

HELEN HALSEY

or

The Swamp State of Conelachita

A TALE OF THE BORDERS

Selected Fiction of William Gilmore Simms
ARKANSAS EDITION

John Caldwell Guilds
EDITOR

THE UNIVERSITY OF ARKANSAS PRESS
FAYETTEVILLE • 1998

02 01 00 99 98   5 4 3 2 1

Designed by Ellen Beeler

⊛ The paper used in this publication meets the minimum requirements of the
American National Standard for Permanence of Paper for Printed Library Materials
Z39.48-1984.

Library of Congress Cataloging-in-Publication Data

Simms, William Gilmore, 1806–1870.
      Helen Halsey, or, The swamp state of Conelachita : a tale of the borders /
John Caldwell Guilds, editor.
          p.   cm. — (Selected fiction of William Gilmore Simms, Arkansas edition)
(The Simms series)
      Includes bibliographical references (p.   ).
      ISBN 1-55728-514-4 (cloth : alk. paper)
      I. Guilds, John Caldwell, 1924–   . II. Title. III. Series. IV. Series: Simms,
William Gilmore, 1806–1870. Selections. 1933.
      PS2848.H3   1998
      813'.54—dc21   97-38272
                                                              CIP

ACKNOWLEDGMENT

I am grateful to Dr. Hilary Harris for her expert work in preparing the text of this book for publication, and for giving me the benefit of her close and perceptive reading of Simms.

CONTENTS

PREFACE TO THE ARKANSAS EDITION*

William Gilmore Simms needs to be read to be appreciated, and he can be neither read nor appreciated unless his works are made available. Thus I am pleased to edit for the University of Arkansas Press *Selected Fiction of William Gilmore Simms: Arkansas Edition*, beginning with *Guy Rivers: A Tale of Georgia*. *Selected Fiction* will include novels originally designated by Simms as Border Romances, selected novels from his Revolutionary War Series, his three novels dealing with pre-colonial and colonial warfare with Native Americans, and several volumes of his best shorter fiction, including *The Wigwam and the Cabin*. In these volumes, Simms depicts the American frontier from pre-colonial times in sixteenth-century Florida in its ever-westward movement across the Appalachian Mountains to the Mississippi River Valley in the early nineteenth century.

Though the Arkansas Edition of Simms will not be a critical edition in the strictest sense, the principles in establishing copy-text are those recommended by the Committee on Scholarly Editions of the Modern Language Association. For each volume copy-text has been selected under the following procedures: (1) if the author issued a revised edition, such edition becomes copy-text; (2) if there was no revised edition, the original publication is the copy-text; (3) if a critical text (established under CEAA or other comparable standards) exists, such text is the copy-text. In each volume of *Selected Fiction* there will be explanatory as well as textual notes, with a list of the more significant substantive revisions made by the author in preparing the text for a revised edition. Simms's nineteenth-century spelling remains unmodernized; all emendations in the text of typographical errors, redundancies, or omissions are recorded.

Each volume will contain both an introduction and an afterword. I am indebted to the University of Arkansas Press for permission to incorporate relevant portions of my *Simms: A Literary Life* for the introductions; the afterwords analyze the works of Simms in more detail and depth than was possible in the limited scope of a biography.

—JCG

*The Preface to the Arkansas Edition and William Gilmore Simms Chronology were originally published in William Gilmore Simms, *Guy Rivers: A Tale of Georgia,* ed. John Caldwell Guilds, Fayetteville: University of Arkansas Press, 1993.

WILLIAM GILMORE SIMMS CHRONOLOGY

1806	Born in Charleston, South Carolina, April 17, the son of William Gilmore Simms, an Irish immigrant, and Harriet Ann Augusta Singleton Simms
1808	Mother died; left in the custody of his maternal grandmother by his father, who, frustrated by personal tragedy and business failure, deserted Charleston for the Southwest
1812–16	Attended public schools in Charleston
1816	At age ten made momentous decision to remain in Charleston with grandmother rather than join now-wealthy father in Mississippi
1816–18	Concluded formal education at private school conducted in buildings of the College of Charleston
1818	Apprenticed to apothecary to explore medical career
1824–25	Visited father in Mississippi; witnessed rugged frontier life
1825	Began study of law in Charleston office of Charles Rivers Carroll; edited (and published extensively in) the *Album*, a Charleston literary weekly
1826	Married Anna Malcolm Giles, October 19
1827	Admitted to bar; appointed magistrate of Charleston; published two volumes of poetry; first child, Anna Augusta Singleton Simms, born November 11
1832	Anna Malcolm Giles Simms died, February 19; made first visit to New York, where he met James Lawson, who became his literary agent and lifelong friend
1833	Published first volume of fiction, *Martin Faber: The Story of a Criminal*
1834	Published first "regular novel," *Guy Rivers: A Tale of Georgia*
1835	Published *The Yemassee: A Tale of Carolina* and *The Partisan: A Tale of the Revolution*

1836   Married Chevillette Eliza Roach, November 15, and moved
            to Woodlands, the plantation owned by her father; published
            Mellichampe: A Legend of the Santee

1837   Birth of Virginia Singleton Simms, November 15; first of
            fourteen children born to Chevillette Roach Simms

1838   Published *Richard Hurdis: or, The Avenger of Blood. A Tale of
            Alabama*

1840   Published *Border Beagles: A Tale of Mississippi* and *The History
            of South Carolina*

1841   Published *The Kinsmen: or, The Black Riders of Congaree:
            A Tale* (later retitled *The Scout*) and *Confession: or, The Blind
            Heart. A Domestic Story*

1842   Published *Beauchampe, or, The Kentucky Tragedy. A Tale of
            Passion* (later retitled *Charlemont*)

1842–43   Editor, *Magnolia*, Charleston literary magazine

1844   Elected to South Carolina legislature for 1844–46 term;
            published *Castle Dismal: or, The Bachelor's Christmas. A
            Domestic Legend*

1845   Published *The Wigwam and the Cabin*, First and Second
            Series; *Helen Halsey: or, The Swamp State of Conelachita. A
            Tale of the Borders;* and *Views and Reviews in American
            Literature, History and Fiction,* First and Second Series; editor,
            Southern and Western (known as "Simms's Magazine")

1846   Published *The Life of Captain John Smith*

1847   Published *The Life of Chevalier Bayard*

1849–54   Editor, *Southern Quarterly Review*

1850   Published *The Lily and the Totem, or, The Huguenots in
            Florida*

1851   Published *Katharine Walton: or, The Rebel of Dorchester. An
            Historical Romance of the Revolution in Carolina* and *Norman
            Maurice; or, The Man of the People, An American Drama*

1852   Published *The Sword and the Distaff; or, "Fair, Fat and Forty," A Story of the South, at the Close of the Revolution* (retitled *Woodcraft*); *The Golden Christmas: A Chronicle of St. John's, Berkeley; As Good as a Comedy; or, The Tennessean's Story;* and *Michael Bonham: or, The Fall of Bexar. A Tale of Texas*

1853   Published *Vasconselos. A Romance of the New World* and a collected edition of *Poems*

1855   Published *The Forayers or the Raid of the Dog-Days*

1856   Published *Eutaw. A Sequel to The Forayers . . . ; Charlemont or The Pride of the Village. A Tale of Kentucky;* and *Beauchampe, or the Kentucky Tragedy. A Sequel to Charlemont;* disastrous lecture tour of North, in which he voiced strong pro-South Carolina and pro-Southern views

1858   Death of two sons to yellow fever on the same day, September 22: the "crowning calamity" of his life

1859   Published *The Cassique of Kiawah. A Colonial Romance*

1860   Vigorously supported the secessionist movement

1862   Woodlands burned; rebuilt with subscription funds from friends and admirers; birth of last child, Charles Carroll Simms, October 20

1863   Chevillette Roach Simms died September 10: "bolt from a clear sky"

1864   Eldest son, William Gilmore Simms, Jr., wounded in Civil War battle in Virginia, June 12; most intimate friend in South Carolina, James Henry Hammond, died November 13

1865   Woodlands burned by stragglers from Sherman's army; witnessed the burning of Columbia, described in *Sack and Destruction of the City of Columbia, S.C.*

1866   Made arduous but largely unsuccessful efforts to reestablish relations with Northern publishers

1867   Published "Joscelyn; A Tale of the Revolution" serially in the magazine *Old Guard*

1869   Published "The Cub of the Panther; A Mountain Legend" serially in *Old Guard;* published "Voltmeier, or the Mountain Men" serially in *Illuminated Western World* magazine

1870   Delivered oration on "The Sense of the Beautiful" May 3; died, after a long bout with cancer, at the Society Street home of his daughter Augusta (Mrs. Edward Roach) in Charleston, June 11, survived by Augusta and five of the fourteen children from his second marriage

INTRODUCTION TO *HELEN HALSEY*

After the publication of *Beauchampe* in 1842, William Gilmore Simms busied himself for several years with editing and politicking and relatively small literary projects, producing in 1843 only *The Social Principle: The True Source of National Prominence: An Oration* (first delivered at the University of Alabama in Tuscaloosa on December 13, 1842, when he was awarded a LL.D. degree);[1] *The Geography of South Carolina* (a companion piece to his earlier *The History of South Carolina*); and *Donna Florida: A Tale*, a slim volume of poetry imitative of Byron. These books elicited little interest and cost their author little labor, being at best occasional pieces or resurrections of earlier efforts. Simms published no fiction during the year, but there is evidence that he was breaking ground, laying the foundation for several major works: during a twelve-month period beginning in November 1844 he brought out in book form two important novelettes, *Castle Dismal* and *Helen Halsey*, and his best collection of short stories, *The Wigwam and the Cabin*.

A question frequently raised about Simms is, Why for a nine-year period extending from 1842 to 1851 did he produce no major full-length novels? Why, in his only long novel between *Beauchampe* (1842) and *Katherine Walton* (1851), did he turn away from his forte—America's struggle for self-identity—to write again on a foreign topic?[2] Why, when he did choose to cover familiar American themes, did he select to write novelettes, short stories, essays, biographies, and poems rather than continue the trend toward success-tested two-volume novels? Despite this apparent error in literary judgment, Simms's imagination did not lie dormant during this period, for he produced in it some of the best writing of his career, albeit none of it in the field of the full-length novel. In short, he did not cease being highly productive, he did not desert familiar American themes, and his concentration on genres other than the novel probably represents his recognition of major changes in American publishing practices rather than a conscious decision to forsake the form through which his reputation had been achieved.

The Panic of 1837, with which a gradual collapse of the national economy began, had devastated the book market by 1843, particularly the sale of the once fashionable, yet costly, two-volume novel. Taking advantage of the absence of an international copyright, the advent of new and rapid printing techniques, and the availability of inexpensively manufactured paper, American publishers for their very survival resorted to "cheap books," paperbound reprints of popular British authors sold at ridiculously low prices, sometimes as low as six cents each. Simms was among the first of American writers to acknowledge the reality of the situation, as his letter of August 16, 1841, to James Henry Hammond reveals:

> Do not . . . suppose that it is easy to get . . . a work published or that . . . writings are now profitable. . . . There are very few American writers who ever get anything. [Joseph Holt] Ingraham could scarcely at this time get a novel published at all—certainly he could hope to get nothing for it. The publishers are very costive—the sales are terribly diminished within the last few years. You will perceive that [Washington] Irving now writes almost wholly for magazines and [James Fenimore] Cooper & myself are almost the only persons whose novels are printed —certainly, we are almost the only persons who hope to get anything for them. From England we get nothing. In this country an Edition now instead of 4 or 5,000 copies, is scarce 2,000. [*L*, I, 271]

Later, in a letter to George Frederick Holmes in October 1843, Simms reiterated: "Novel writing is not encouraging by its results & beyond a few short stories I have done nothing in that way for some time" (*L*, I, 379). Simms's early and accurate perception of what was happening in the publishing industry almost certainly influenced his choice of genre during the middle and late 1840s, though it did not affect his long-range commitment to writing novels on American historical themes.

Certainly, with the exception of *Count Julian* and his ill-advised (yet often reprinted) biography of Francis Marion,[3] there was no falloff in the quality of his published works beginning in 1844. Simms first focused upon "Castle Dismal," one of several excellent stories of his to appear in the *Magnolia* in 1842, deciding in late 1843 to make it "a small vol. of 150 pages or thereabout" (*L*, I, 369). *Castle Dismal: or, The Bachelor's Christmas* (New York: Burgess, Stringer, 1844), which won the immediate admiration of no less acute critic than Edgar Allan Poe,[4] showed Simms in a vein in which he at times excelled—the supernatural story of manners. Even more laudatory than Poe's was the review written by critic Evert A. Duyckinck for the *New York Morning News* of November 9, 1844:

> If it be any merit in a ghost-story to arrest the reader's attention at the first moment of perusal, and hold it fixed page after page, chapter after chapter, through one hour, two hours to the fitting time of midnight till candle and story go out together, then is Castle Dismal one of the best ghost stories we ever read. The story is well told by Mr. Simms, an adept in this species of narrative. We question whether there is anywhere a better manager in the construction of a tale, who can take such

simple unexaggerated material and make so much of it. . . . Simms still relies upon character and passion and literally takes the reader by storm by the downright force and reality of his action.

Despite its praise by contemporaries like Poe and Duyckinck, *Castle Dismal,* like much of Simms's best work, has been neglected by present-day scholars and critics. It deserves a better fate: in establishing atmosphere, tone, and mood it is superb; setting and characterization deftly contribute to "the willing suspension of disbelief" essential in protraying the supernatural. As late as 1863 Simms (a better critic of his fiction than his poetry) listed *Castle Dismal* as one of his favorite works, one of those he sought to have republished.[5]

The publication of *Castle Dismal* was closely followed by that of another Simms novelette, *Helen Halsey: or, The Swamp State of Conelachita. A Tale of the Borders,* also issued in New York by Burgess, Stringer. Simms first mentioned "Ellen Halsey, or my Wife against my Will" in a June 12, 1843, letter to his New York friend and literary agent James Lawson; at that time the author was proposing it to Harper & Brothers as part of "a collection of Tales of the South," and in a show of financial desperation, he added, "I am willing that they should try the experiment with a cheap edition, sharing half the profits" (*L*, I, 353–54). By the end of September Simms informed Lawson that the "nearly ready" manuscript of "'Helen Halsey . . .' a Border Story—a tale of Mississippi" should best be considered a separate publication, a companion piece to *Castle Dismal* (*L*, I, 369). With his friend Lawson as his agent, Simms attempted to play one publisher against another, Benjamin against Harper (see *L*, I, 381, 390), an unsuccessful manipulation which led to Lawson's offering *Helen Halsey* (as well as *Castle Dismal*) to Burgess, Stringer,[6] the eventual publisher. But the new "Border Story" did not appear until January 1845, two months after *Castle Dismal.* Simms was annoyed that Stringer had not published *Helen Halsey* earlier—before *Castle Dismal*—for upon the latter's publication, he wrote Lawson: "I am sorry that Burgess & Stringer put forth this story first, for I think 'Helen Halsey' much the best, and they promised otherwise" (*L*, I, 436).

Perhaps because of the timing—that is, one book almost immediately following another, both by the same author and publisher—*Helen Halsey* was not reviewed so widely or so favorably as was *Castle Dismal.* A brief notice of "this most attractive and thrilling romance by our talented townsman" appeared in the *Charleston Southern Patriot* of January 2, 1845; and, before its date of publication, Duyckinck anticipated *Helen Halsey*'s arrival by recapitulating its plot for the benefit of future readers (*New York Morning News,* November 29, 1844). Despite the fact that no major journal, Northern or Southern, singled out *Helen Halsey* for critique,[7] Simms reported to E. A. Duyckinck that "Here, in Carolina" the book had "sold well" and that "here the favorable opinions of many of our best men console me" (*L,* II, 20). Simms always had a special fondness for *Helen Halsey;* in late June 1844, he had written Lawson that his new "Border Story" "is very superior" to *Count Julian* (a comparison not necessarily indicative of high praise), and added, "Indeed, as a rapid and truthful domestic story I think it one of my most successful performances. Besides, its style is, I am disposed to believe, particularly good" (*L,* I, 420).

Helen Halsey, it is interesting to note, follows a trend in Simms's Border Romances to highlight marital conflict as well as physical violence in frontier life. Like *Beauchampe* and *Confession* immediately before it in the series, *Helen Halsey* is a "tale of passion" in which the heroine is exploited and victimized in a domestic situation from which there is no escape. The teenage daughter of a well-meaning but weak father who collaborates in crime with the outlaw gang ruled by his vicious and vindictive brother, Helen Halsey is forced by her uncle into marriage with her lover, who has followed her into the "swamp state of Conelachita," the brotherhood's extensive, well-guarded, almost impregnable hide-out presumably located within the borders of Mississippi and/or Louisiana. The purpose of the marriage, performed by a corrupt Episcopal priest who is a member of the gang, is to ensure the loyalty of the couple and prevent their return to civilization, where they might disclose the bandits' operations and whereabouts. Thus, though happy to be married to each other, Henry Meadows (the first-person narrator and protagonist) and "his outlaw's daughter-bride" are virtual prisoners of the gang, and during their attempted escape Helen is killed by her own uncle. *Helen Halsey'*s strengths lie in its fast-moving, action-filled narration; its vivid imagery in the descriptions of the lush, dense swampland wilderness; and its especially graphic portrayal of the modus operandi of the criminal network that had indeed ruthlessly dominated much of the Southwestern frontier in the early nineteenth century. That the organization included rough, profane women who actively participated in assault and robbery and that the Bud Halsey brotherhood possessed an in-kind chaplain to conduct weddings, funerals, and other "Christian" services for its membership were particularly dramatic revelations for readers of the day and constituted new and innovative subject matter for the American novel.

Perhaps the best drawn character in the short novel is Mowbray, the intellectual, aristocratic, resentful, egotistical Episcopal divine who had deserted his wife, child, and church to pursue a life of dissipation and crime, first in New Orleans and then in the swamp kingdom. Simms's self-centered priest—who preaches more effectively after sinning, eventually confesses and repents of his hypocrisy, and dies in a willful act of penitence asking for God's mercy and forgiveness—anticipates Hawthorne's Dimmesdale in *The Scarlet Letter* by five years. Since it is known that Hawthorne read (and reviewed) Simms's *Views and Reviews* in 1846, the question arises if he could also have taken mental note of *Helen Halsey,* published only a few months earlier.[8] Probably there was no direct influence; despite parallels in the behavior of Mowbray and Dimmesdale, each is his own character, the creation of the individual author. In any case Simms's characterization of Mowbray, perhaps the first basically sympathetic portrayal of an introspective, unsaintly priest in the American novel, is striking enough to stand on its own merits.

Notes

1. *The Social Principle* was published in Tuscaloosa by the Erosophic Society of the University of Alabama; *The Geography of South Carolina* in Charleston by Babcock; and *Donna Florida* in Charleston by Burges & James.

2. *Count Julian; or, the Last Days of the Goth: A Historical Romance* was published in Baltimore and New York by William Taylor in 1845. Having conceived of the idea of a story "founded on the apostacy of Count Julian" when "I was 17–18," Simms had begun work on *Count Julian* again in 1838 or 1839, but the unfinished manuscript was lost for at least two years (see *L*, I, 142n) before Simms recovered it and decided to "bestir myself with the conclusion" (Simms to Lawson, January 6, 1845; *L*, II, 12). Simms dedicated the book to John Pendleton Kennedy, who graciously acknowledged the honor in a letter of March 18, 1846 (*L*, II, 159–60n). Willis Gaylord Clark, however, in a scathing review of *Count Julian*, sarcastically chided Simms for linking a worthy name to an unworthy book (*Knickerbocker* 27 [April 1846]: 356–57).

An interesting anecdote, one of several concerned with the author's psychic experiences, centers on the "loss" of the *Count Julian* manuscript. According to family tradition, Simms was advised by a spiritual medium near the New York docks not to travel from New York to Charleston on a certain ship on which he had already booked passage. Simms consequently cancelled his passage, but was unable to retrieve the manuscript. "The ship did go down off Cape Hatteras and *Count Julian* was washed up somewhere on the shores and was finally published" (*MCSO*, I). In 1841 Simms referred to the manuscript of *Count Julian* as "the work which was lost so long & has now only recently been restored to me" (*L*, I, 281).

3. *The Life of Francis Marion* (New York: Henry G. Langley, 1844) was rather widely (and at times favorably) reviewed; but, other than providing its author with excellent background for his Revolutionary Romances, it has little literary value. It should be noted, however, that from a historical viewpoint, Simms has received recognition as a biographer. See Edward H. O'Neill, *A History of American Biography, 1800–1935* (Philadelphia, 1935), 29–30, 54; J. W. Webb, "Simms as Biographer," *University of Mississippi Studies in English* 2 (1961): 111–24; and Peter L. Shillingsburg, "The Uses of Sources in Simms's Biography of Francis Marion" (master's thesis, University of South Carolina, 1967).

4. In his review of *The Wigwam and the Cabin*, Poe has high praise for Simms as an author and lists *Castle Dismal* among his "best fictions" (*Broadway Journal* 2 [October 4, 1845]: 190–91). Trent was impressed that Poe "praised this story highly, and as its theme lay in Poe's own province, his opinion is entitled to carry much weight"; but Trent added that "a modern reader, however, might be inclined to set less store by the supernatural portions of the story than by the description of the old homestead from which it took its name" (p. 150).

5. See his letter of January 10, 1863, to John Rueben Thompson, *L*, IV, 420.

6. Simms to Lawson, February 15, 1844: "You are quite at liberty to dispose of the other tale [*Helen Halsey*] at the same price [as *Castle Dismal*] to Stringer. My object is to get them off of my hands without positively giving them away" (*L*, I, 404). Apparently Simms received a hundred dollars apiece for the two books; on April 30, 1844, he stated to Lawson, "I should like to get my $100 for the latter" (*L*, I, 416–17).

7. Note, however, that Poe included *Helen Halsey* among Simms's "best fictions" in his famous review of *The Wigwam and the Cabin* in the *Broadway Journal* for October 4, 1845.

8. Hawthorne's review of *Views and Reviews in American Literature, History and Fiction* (New York: Wiley and Putnam, 1845) that appeared in the *Salem Advertiser* of May 2, 1846, is reprinted in Randall Stewart, "Hawthorne's Contributions to *The Salem Advertiser*," *American Literature* 5 (January 1934): 327–41—unequivocal evidence of Hawthorne's reading of Simms. In an important, as yet unpublished study of *Castle Dismal*, Renee Dye points out striking similarities between Simms's portrayal of an adulterous clergyman in *Castle Dismal* and Hawthorne's delineation of Dimmesdale—demonstrating that *Helen Halsey* is not the only work by Simms that perhaps anticipates *The Scarlet Letter*.

HELEN HALSEY,

OR

THE SWAMP STATE OF CONELACHITA:

A TALE OF THE BORDERS.

~~~~~~~~

BY W. GILMORE SIMMS,

AUTHOR OF "RICHARD HURDIS," "THE YEMASSEE,"
"THE KINSMEN," &C.

~~~~~~~~

NEW-YORK:

BURGESS, STRINGER & CO.

222 Broadway, corner of Ann street.

BOSTON: Redding & Co. PHILADELPHIA: G. B. Zeiber & Co.

1845.

HELEN HALSEY:

OR,

THE SWAMP STATE OF CONELACHITA.

A TALE OF THE BORDERS.

BY W. GILMORE SIMMS,

AUTHOR OF "RICHARD HURDIS," "THE YEMASSEE," "THE
KINSMEN," &C.

"Even so it was with me when I was young;
If we are Nature's, these are ours: this thorn
Doth to our rose of youth rightly belong;
Our blood to us, this to our blood is born;
It is the show and seal of Nature's truth,
Where Love's strong passion is imprest in youth:
By our remembrances of days foregone,
Such were our faults,—O! then we thought them none."

SHAKSPEARE.

NEW-YORK:

BURGESS, STRINGER & CO.

1845.

J.R. WINSER, PRINTER, 29 ANN-STREET.

RANDELL HUNT, ESQ.

OF LOUISIANA

My Dear Randell:

   I am reminded, in putting forth this little volume, of the friendly interest which you took, nearly twelve years ago, in the fortunes of another work of similar dimensions——my first experiment in prose literature, Martin Faber,——which was then issued from the press. The inscription of the present volume with your name, may serve to recal, not unpleasantly to your memory, with the circumstances of that period, the recollection of

THE AUTHOR.

New-York, Oct. 1, 1844

CHAPTER ONE

The unwise license and injurious freedoms accorded to youth in our day and country, will render it unnecessary to explain how it was that, with father and mother, a good homestead, and excellent resources, I was yet suffered at the early age of eighteen, to set out on a desultory and almost purposeless expedition, among some of the wildest regions of the South-West. It would be as unnecessary and, perhaps, much more difficult, to show what were my own motives in undertaking such a journey. A truant disposition, a love of adventure, or, possibly, the stray glances of some forest maiden, may all be assumed as good and sufficient reasons, to set a warm heart wandering, and provoke wild impulses in the blood of one, by nature impetuous enough, and, by education, very much the master of his own will. With a proud heart, hopeful of all things if thoughtless of any, as noble a steed as ever shook a sable mane over a sunny prairie, and enough money, liberally calculated, to permit an occasional extravagance, whether in excess or charity, I set out one sunny winter's morning from *Leaside,* our family place, carrying with me the tearful blessings of my mother, and as kind a farewell from my father, as could decently comport with the undis-guised displeasure with which he had encountered the first expression of my wish to go abroad. Well might he disapprove of a determination which was so utterly without an object. But our discussion on this point need not be resumed. Enough, that, if "my path was all before me," I was utterly without a guide. It was, besides, my purpose to go where there were few if any paths; regions as wild as they were pathless; among strange tribes and races; about whose erring and impulsive natures we now and then heard such tales of terror, and of wonder, as carried us back to the most venerable periods of feudal history, and seemed to promise us a full return and realization of their strangest and saddest legends. Of stories such as these, the boy sees only the wild and picturesque aspects,—such as are beautiful with a startling beauty—such as impress his imagination rather than his thoughts, and presenting the truth to his eyes through the medium of his fancies, divest it of whatever is coarse, or cold, or cruel, in its composition. It was thus that I had heard of these things, and thus that, instead of repelling, as they would have done, robbed of that charm of distance which equally beautifies in the moral as in the natural world, they invited my footsteps, and seduced me from the more appropriate domestic world in which my lot had been cast.

With a light heart, full of expectation, a free steed that seemed rather to swim along through space, than tread monotonously over the rugged ground, the day passed away with an almost unnoted flight. My eyes had been charmed in the observation of trees and groves, picturesque objects of sight in hill and dale, wood and water, and such occasional more worldly matters, as were provoked by long ranges of whitened cotton fields, or yellow corn yet bristling in unbroken rows. At the close of the day, I had reached a cabin where I found shelter for the night, and at early dawn, I again set forth, with the promise of another day of generous sunshine. This day was consumed like the last, and with equal satisfaction to myself. The buoyant spirit of youth rises in exultation in any exercise, which seems to impart equal freedom to soul and body; and there is something of the same triumphant pulse in the heart, galloping over the prairies, over the hills, or through the long cathedral ranges of gigantic pine forests, which one feels on the deck of a fine ship, careering over the billows of the broad Atlantic, with a breeze that sends the foam flying at every plunge, from the bold prow of the imperial vessel. The man is wonderfully lifted with the consciousness of having at his command, and being able to command, such a noble animal as the horse, and rapidity of motion is the source of an intoxication, of a sublime sort, of the character of which we can form a good conception from the interest we take in a race, whether of steeds or steamboats; the danger of being hurled down by the one or blown up by the other, being, in both cases, absolutely and entirely forgotten. Mine was a nature particularly to exult in such exercises, my temperament being wholly sanguine, and the indulgence of my parents having left it to an unrestrained exercise, which rendered it feverishly irritable when not engaged in such performances as were grateful to my excitable imagination. After the close of the second day of my journey, it seemed to me as if both my horse and self could have begun anew, with a more buoyant spirit than before,—if the toil itself refreshed us, and as if no more grateful object lay before us, than just be permitted to be wander on, and on,—"the world forgetting, by the world forgot." Certainly, the true secret of perpetual life, is perpetual motion. Find the one, and we secure the other. Alas! the want of *daylight,* is the great drawback to our progress and discoveries. We have just begun to make them when the curtain falls upon us.

The close of the second day brought me to the foot of a long range of hills, the lower steps possibly of the great Apalachian chain, inclining to the Mississippi. It also brought me to the very borders of what was in that day, known as the region of doubt and shadow. I had reached the confines of civilization—even such imperfect civilization as belonged to our thinly settled frontiers. I was now ninety miles from Leaside, and only separated by a narrow wall of hills from that strange region of forest mystery and romance, about which so many surprising stories had been told me. This also was the Indian country—here the red men still lingered, mixed up with reckless, renegade whites, who preferred the wild privileges of savage, to the more wholesome, but seemingly less attractive pleasures, of civilized life. As I thought over this taste, I could not but shudder to discover that such also, to some extent, was the feeling in my own bosom. But I was too young to encourage unpleasant reflections, and for these but little time was allowed me. Just on the edge of this neutral ground—this debateable land—neither savage nor social—stood a house that has since had more than one remarkable history. It was a miserable shell of logs, roughly hewn, of two stories, to which, in the rear, was appended a long shed of frame-work, intended to contain some three chambers, or, upon a press of company—passage way included—possibly four. It was a *public* of notorious resort—standing almost astride the area, from which diverged four roads, leading to as many different quarters of country. It was consequently much frequented, and the landlord, who will probably be well remembered by many as Jephson Yannaker, was, at the time of which I speak, doing a thriving business. There were many witless lads like myself, travelling for their humors, and many more, not so witless, but more reckless, travelling in the same regions—at our expense. I had not much time allowed me to examine the exterior of this establishment, before a stout, shock-headed, burly, red-faced, but kindly looking personage, whom I soon learned to be Yannaker himself, advanced from the door-way to the head of my horse.

"Come, 'light, stranger,—you're just in time to shake a leg with the best of them. 'Light! I'll see to the critter."

His words were explained a moment after, as the discordant twang of a half-tuned fiddle smote my ears from the interior. In entering, I had just time to discover that several horses were hitched to neighboring trees, and on one side of the premises, but rather nearer to the house, there stood a sort of travelling carriage of rude structure—a strong, unwieldy vehicle, to which two able draught horses were still partially attached. From a few bundles of fodder at their feet, it seemed to be the design of their driver, who was busy in the carriage, that they should enjoy their forage where they stood.

But the sight within made me forget every thing without. The hall ran nearly the whole length of the building, and it was comparatively a large one. A bright fire was blazing in the chimney, and a matter of thirty persons, or even more, were strewn around the apartment. Of these, though less than half, a fair proportion were women. Near the fire sat the fiddler, the croakings and creakings of whose crazy instrument had assaulted me on my first arrival. He was still busy in the seemingly hopeless task of screwing its strings into something like symphonious exercise and utterance. He was a plain country lad, in homespun, with a cap of coonskin still clinging to his head, which swung pendulously over his fiddle, as he now jerked at the keys, and now jostled with the bow.

But there was nothing in his appearance calculated to detain my glance. This now roved about the assembly, which promised to be as interesting as it was certainly promiscuous and picturesque. The men were stout fellows all, of the true farm-yard breed, famous at the flail, and with fists, whose seeming efficiency reminded me more than once of the powers ascribed to those of Maximin, the Gaul, who could fell a bullock at a blow. It did not seem as if they had prepared themselves for the festivities they were about to enjoy. Their costume was that of the farm-yard. Plain blue or yellow home-spun, rough shoes, and, though the winter had fairly set in, many were the bronzed and naked breasts displayed by the open shirt of coarse cotton. The frolic, so far as they were concerned, was evidently *extempore*. They had been suffered no time for the toilet. But this did not seem greatly to abash them. The unconventional world in which they lived, had rendered them somewhat insensible to that feeling of *mauvaise honte*, which would have been sure, in such a case, to have distressed the half civilized lad to all immeasurable extent. They showed no concern at the matter, but dashed forward, each to his favorite lass, as coolly and confidently as if fashion had received her dues, and the toilet all the necessary sacrifices. And there was, in this very freedom, a sort of savage grace, which greatly tended to lessen the rudeness of its general aspects. Most of the fellows were well formed—rough, but erect and easy—and having that use of their limbs, boldly flexible, which the life of the hunter and the horseman is very apt to impart in the case of a well made person. Where had these lads come from? From a space of country twenty miles round, through which the very whispers of a fiddle make themselves heard, heaven knows how, and whose attractions among such a people are felt, heaven only knows to what extent. Some of them were professional hunters; some, idle ramblers like myself; and some few might have been gathered in the immediate neighborhood. But, as I could give no very good reason for my own presence in such a place, it would be unreasonable to expect me to account for theirs.

The girls,—but here the case is very different. When did ever damsel find herself in such a situation without contriving some of her secret graces before the toilet? Though she mirrors her beauties in the stream, she will yet manage to give them some of those helps of art, a knowledge of which she seems to have caught by instinct. There were some twelve or fourteen damsels in the room, and a profusion of ribbons—and of these a country girl must have the gaudiest. Fancy, gentle reader, the picture for yourself. See Mary with her bandeau of Hibernian green—her belt of golden yellow—her neckerchief that seems to have been dyed in summer rainbows, and her dress that might have been made out of their skirts. And there is Susan in her head dress, and Sally in her blue and scarlet, and Jenny in her "Jim-along-Josey," without ever dreaming that her style of body garment would ever become a fashion in the great city, and be known by such an imposing name. I am not good at such details, and you must conceive them for yourself. It is very certain, however, that, with all their superior pains-taking at the toilet, the women lacked the graces—however inferior—which distinguished the deportment of the men. They sat, stiffly and awkwardly, like so many waxen figures, each on her stool, as if troubled with a disquieting apprehension that any unwise movement would over-turn the fair fabric of her present state, and be equally fatal to headdress, handkerchief and happiness. There was one exception to this uniform display of ostentation and awkwardness,—of whom more hereafter.

But the waxen images were made to move. The fiddle began to speak in tolerable tune, and the brawny boys sprang across the ocean of floor that separated them from the green beauties on the sunny banks, and appro-priated them, I suppose, according to previous arrangement. In the twin-kling of an eye they were upon the ground, every mother's son of them, and busy in the mazes of the country dance. Such a shuffling of feet, such a tearing of music to very tatters, by that crazy violin, and the inveterate musician, who scraped away as if catgut could bring about the noblest catastrophe,—would require the creation of a special muse to describe, and, until that event, we leave the affair to the quick conception and conjecture of the reader.

CHAPTER TWO

I know not why, but the whole proceeding, with all its whirl and excitement, its odd merriment and grotesque display of art, produced in me a feeling of disquiet, approaching even to melancholy. Perhaps, this was because it reminded me of Leaside, and the fiddling of old Ben, our venerable butler, when little Mary Bonham was my partner, and we wandered down together in the same sweet primitive movements that now seemed to be desecrated wantonly before my eyes. The whole scene of home grew up before me as I gazed and mused. The stately hall, hung with pictures, nicely curtained, with the massive piano on one side, and the equally massive book-case on the other; the one a treasury of the sweetest sounds, the other of the noblest sense. My father, with his white hairs, on one side of the fireplace; my mother, with her stiffly-starched white cap on the other;—the one with his huge Shakspeare on the little table beside him,—closed, with his silver spectacles peeping out between the leaves;—the other with her knitting apparatus in her lap, the work dropping to her feet, as she watched our movements, while the kitten, lying on its back, was disentangling with mischievous painstaking that which had tasked the ingenuity and industry of the good old dame, to put together, for the last half dozen evenings. That passing but sweet glimpse of the dear old homestead, with all its holy associations, was the first mental image which crossed my mind, reproachful of my wanderings. You may be sure I did not encourage it, but, anxious to remove it, I hastened round the dancers, to the opposite side, intending to make my escape at the doorway, and go out beneath the skies; but I was interrupted in this progress, and diverted from this purpose, by finding the narrow way occupied. I looked down at the person who thus obstructed my pathway, and almost recoiled in pleasurable surprise. Before me sat a young girl of fifteen or thereabouts. She certainly could not have been more than sixteen. The first thing that struck me about her was the exquisite but dewy brightness of her eye, which was as dark of hue as the coal may be supposed to be on the eve of that moment, when, under the force of heat, it becomes a brilliant. The face was small, very small, when you turned suddenly from the blaze of the large expanding eye to note the accompanying features;—but it was also very beautiful. The skin was singularly clear and transparent for such black eyes and hair. The forehead, about which was bound a narrow braid, was high and broad, and constituted fully one half of the face. The hair was parted, madonna fashion, as if art, after long experience, had become assured that, in the present case, her best policy was to obey the laws of simplicity. Her neck, which was only half bared, seemed very white and beautifully rounded. Her figure, which was evidently slight, could not be distinguished, by reason of the huge travelling cloak in which she was still wrapped. The whole appearance of this young creature, so unique, yet so little like the rest in the assembly, fixed my regard, and would have done so even had the excessive brilliancy of her eyes and beauty of her complexion not enchained it. Her seeming isolation, too, so much like my own, was another circumstance to commend her to my sympathies. A scene like the present, in a frontier country, I need not say to my readers, is apt to set at defiance the more restraining laws of society in the obviously social world; and, assuming the exercise of one of the most understood privileges of the place, I did not hesitate to accost the stranger. She was evidently a stranger like myself, and I jumped at once to the conclusion that she was one of the inmates of the travelling carriage that I had seen at the door.

"You do not dance," I said to her, bending down beside her, and speaking in those subdued tones which seem the properest when addressing the young, the timid and the artless.

She looked up, then around her, with something of the expression of a startled fawn, away from its dam, and trembling at the approach of some strange monster of the wilderness. There was an air of anxiety in her glance, which made me more cautious in my approaches, and at the same time, more earnest in my interest. As she did not answer, I put my inquiry in another shape.

"Will you not dance with me?"

"Oh, no!" she answered, still looking anxiously around her, and particularly at the entrance,—"Oh, no! I do not wish to dance. I am a stranger here,—I know nobody."

"I too am a stranger here," was my reply—"let us therefore know one another—let us be friends."

She allowed her eyes to rise for a moment to the level of mine, and when they encountered my glance, a deep crimson overspread her cheek.

"Shall we not be friends?" I repeated, as I found she did not design to answer.

"What can I do?" she answered; and the question struck me as remarkable for its simplicity. It seemed to indicate a higher standard of duty, in the matter of friendship, on the part of this young creature, than was customary among mankind in general. I contrived, however, to reply, though her question was evidently one not easy of answer.

"What should a friend do, but love his friend, and think of him, and pray for him, and be glad to see him, and sorry to lose him."

"Ah! but I shall soon be gone."

"Gone! where?"

"To my own home—you to yours."

"And why should we go different ways?"

"I don't know," she said, in slow, subdued tones, which so far flattered me, as they seemed to be regretful ones.

"There is no reason why we should not go together, at least for a little while. For my part, I have set out to travel, and it does not matter much whither I go. Where do you live?"

"Miles off—very far. Close by the river—"

"River—what river?"

"Far—far! You cannot go. No, no! You cannot go there."

I observed, as she replied, that her glances sought anxiously the entrance, before which I now discovered, in the dim light of evening, that there stood a group of persons, three or four in number.

"You little know how far I am willing to go for my friend—for those whom I love;" was my reply, and my hand rested, while I spoke, unconsciously on my own part, on hers. I felt hers tremble beneath it—withdrawn—and only then was I conscious of the trespass, which, had I been in a highly civilized world, had been committed by this presumption. I proceeded:

"If one's friend is true and worthy, one follows her to the end of the world, follows nobody else, thinks of nobody else, cares for nobody else, loves her over all the world."

"Ah! that is friendship;" she answered with a sigh.

"I would be your friend—I will follow you;" I continued impetuously, encouraged by her words.

"No! no!—I have no friend. I live very far,—by the river—the road is hard to find—bad swamps—you cannot follow me."

Her answer was made with some trepidation, and an increased anxiety of expression, as her glance was directed towards the door.

"And why should it be hard to find, and why should the bad roads and the swamps prevent me, when it does not prevent you? Why can't I follow you? I *will* follow you."

"No, *you must not!—As a friend* you must not."

This was spoken with singular emphasis; then she paused abruptly, as if disquieted at the degree of *empressement* which she had given to her utterance. But she had also given peculiar force to the word "*friend*," and *that* pleased me. It seemed to say that she herself was not displeased with the appropriation. But there was a mystery in the whole matter. Her strange mode of speech—so artless, yet so reserved—her evident anxiety, if not apprehension,—and the secrecy—could it spring from ignorance —which she resolutely maintained as to the whereabouts of her abode? I was resolved not to give the matter up. But, for that moment, this resolution was made in vain. We were interrupted, and, as I thought, rather rudely, by some one thrusting himself in between us. I turned to meet the intruder, in a mood prompt enough to punish the intrusion, and was confronted by the stern glance of a man in middle life—perhaps a little beyond it—such seemed the testimony afforded by thick masses of grisly beard which stood about his cheeks and chin. His keen, inquiring glance, fixed upon my own face, rather tended to increase the disposition which I felt to resent what I esteemed his impertinence, but the momentary reflection that he might be the father of the damsel, moved me to tolerate a bearing which, under any other circumstances, would have moved me to do battle, and which, in the opinion of the country, would not only have justified, but called for it. While I was meditating what to say,—for he still kept his glance fixed upon me—the girl rose and took his arm. He turned from me at this instant and led her off to an adjoining apartment, followed by Yannaker, the host, who seemed to be busy in no worse office than that of showing the parties their several chambers.

"My game is up for the night!" was my muttered reflection, and, so thinking, I dashed out of the hall, and with hot brow and excited spirit, stood, unknowing where to turn, beneath the cool and mantling starlight.

CHAPTER THREE

The sounds of that crazy violin, which I now began again to hear, sounded a worse discord in my ears than ever, and gave an impulse to my footsteps which they seemed to need. I dashed forward, following what seemed the opened grounds, and soon found myself ascending a little range of hills. The night was very clear and very beautiful,—of that sombrous sort of beauty when the light just suffices to enable you to distinguish objects, but helps, at the same time, to magnify their aspects by its own vague medium. The trees stood up,—those stately pines which maintain, day and night, one unceasing murmur, which is more dear than song to the imaginative spirit—in frowning and vast magnificence beside me, like so many gigantic wardens of the land, marshalling the entrance to some wondrous palace. Under their guidance, as it were, and through their ranks, I hurried on, musing over the thousand fancies which, I suppose, would be natural enough to any youth under the same circumstances—newly enriched by a sense of liberty—a feeling of manliness—which the very privilege of roving at that hour, and in new scenes, would be apt to inspire;—and, anon, reproached by the stern internal monitor within, for filial disobe-dience,—remembering, with sinking heart, the tears of my mother, and the frowning farewell of my father—all of which was, in another moment, to be banished from thought, by the intrusive image of that strange, sweet maiden, sitting by herself, wrapped up in her heavy cloak, yet looking out with such bright, diamond-like, heart-conducting eyes. I might have wandered thus for hours, perhaps all night, for what youth with such feel-ings in his heart, and such ferment in his brain, ever cares for the dull sleep of ordinary mortals,—had I not been roused to other thoughts by a sudden and startling sound, which reached me from the range of dark hills opposite. I could only liken this sound, with which I was unfamiliar, to the

bay or howl of the wolf, or perhaps, a dozen of them; and though the idea
of a wolf-hunt struck me the next moment, as being among the most
famous of all ideas, it was some qualification, just then, to any such desire,
that I was horseless, weaponless, without company, and totally ignorant of
the habits of the animal, and the country in which I stood. That domestic
virtue, discretion, interposing at this juncture, persuaded me to retrace my
steps to Yannaker's, which I reached in reasonable time, after once
measuring my length over a stump, that very imprudently stood in my way
on the slope of a little hillock. The violin was still at work, and though I
felt apprehensive that, until it slept, I should not,—I persuaded old
Yannaker out of the circle, where he himself shook a leg, in order that he
should show me the way to my chamber—a measure to which I was
induced, by being convinced that the fair stranger would not again emerge
from hers that night.

I slept soon and soundly, in spite of my convictions—slept to dream,
precisely as I had mused, of home, and strange woods and adventures,
with, ever and anon, that fair young face, and those dark lustrous eyes,
peering downward, as if from heaven into my very heart. This image so
completely filled my brain, that it was the first to encounter me at my
waking. I started up with a bright sun blazing through a half-opened
window upon me. There was a stir below, and, half vexed with myself for
having slept so late, I jumped out of bed and ran to the open window. As
I feared the travelling carriage had disappeared, and in it, as I concluded,
my fair incognita. I dressed myself with all despatch, and hurried below.
Preparations for breakfast were in progress, though the room still retained
some of the traces of last night's exertions. Part of an antique frill lay in
one place at my feet, and at a little distance I detected beneath the breakfast table a stripe of red stuff, most like red flannel, in conjecturing the uses
of which I was reminded of the apocryphal story of the Countess of
Salisbury, and the now proverbial sentence of the courteous monarch,—
'Honi soit qui mal y pense.' The worst evil that I was thinking of, was my
mysterious damsel, and the timely entrance of Yannaker enabled me to
make the necessary inquiries.

"Gone, sir—gone as fast as a pair of the best horses in Massassipp could
carry her."

"How long, Mr. Yannaker?"

"Don't mister me, *stranger*,—I'm plain Jeph Yannaker to travellers, and
Yannaker to them that knows me. I'm agin making a handle for a man's
name before you can trust yourself to take hold of it."

"No offence, Jeph Yannaker—I only speak as I've been accustomed."

"No offence, to be sure,—it's your teaching, stranger, but here in our parts, where people's scarce, and the sight of one's neighbor does the heart good, a handle to his name seems to push him too far out of the reach of a friendly gripe. It's a stiff, cold sort of business, this mistering and squiring—will do well enough among mere gentlemen, and lawyers, and judges, and such sort of cattle,—but out here, where a look upon the hills and swamps seems to give a man a sort of freedom, it's a God's blessing that we have few such people here. Here we're nothing but men, just as God made us,—not to speak of a little addition, in the shape of jacket and breeches, made out of blue or yellow homespun."

Those who have had the good fortune to know Jeph Yannaker will give me credit for having reported him correctly. His life was an eventful one, and, one day, shall have its history, though it come from no better hand than my own. But to return. After some little time taken up in disclaimers and other matters,—for it seemed to me as if the worthy publican was wilfully bent on avoiding the topic to which I sought to confine his attention, —I at length gathered from him, not only that the damsel had taken her departure, but that she had been gone ever since midnight—that she never slept in the house at all, but had only retired, with her uncle, from the crowd—that, as soon as the moon rose, the latter had geared his horses, and just when I was enjoying the sweetest dreams of the treasure so newly found, she was spirited away by her grisly protector—whom I rejoiced to find was not her father—but, in what direction, Yannaker either could not or would not say. I immediately declared my purpose to pursue, and requested that he would have my horse brought out. He looked at me with open mouth, and a chuckling "haw! haw! haw!"—that promised to correspond with the boundless dimensions of his distended throat. I became impatient, and with some peevishness demanded the occasion of so much unreasonable and unseasonable merriment.

"What!—go?" he asked.

"Yes, sir,—go! and what is there so very laughable in such a determination?"

He composed his muscles instantly.

"Not before breakfast,—oh! no!—I'm sure of you till then. Why, breakfast is a good thing, the best of things on an empty stomach—breakfast is a warm thing, the warmest of things for a winter day. Why, stranger, no man's brains do good service, unless breakfast has warmed his belly; and, I tell you, even the horse, besides, knows when his master is well filled and sensible, and when he is not. Let a good horse alone for that. Why, lad, the best horse I ever knew or crossed, would always cut capers when a man undertook to straddle him who happened to be hungry; no horse of mine should ever be crossed, if I know'd it, by a man who hadn't had his breakfast."

"It so happens, Mr. Yannaker—"

"Plain Yannaker—plain Yannaker," he said interrupting me.

"Well, then, plain Yannaker—"

"Ha! ha! ha! That's it. You're right—I like you the better for it. Say 'plain Yannaker,' if you please, in preference to Mister Yannaker."

"I say, then, plain Yannaker, that my horse is not yours, and neither knows nor cares whether I have had my breakfast or not."

"Wouldn't have such a horse, stranger, as a gift. By the Lord Harry, I wouldn't. But don't be wolfish at Jeph Yannaker. Here's your breakfast, and your horse shall follow it, as soon after as you please—only, let me tell you you're clean mistaken. Never was a horse yet that didn't know whether his master was fed or not—unless he was an idiot beast—a clear senseless animal,—and I reckon there may be idiot beasts as well as idiot men. There now,—sit down to your breakfast,—the old woman's poured out the coffee, and all's ready. I'll see to the critter."

Jeph Yannaker had a way of his own, as most who knew him know, which there was no resisting. He had the most good humored cast of countenance, the most benevolent smile, the most kind solicitude of manner,—yet, if tales speak true, he could cut a purse, and a throat too upon occasion, as promptly as the Pacha of Yannina. Of this, however, in another history. Enough, for the reader, that I, a boy of eighteen, found it impossible to be angry with such a person, and he forty-five or fifty. He quieted me in the most persuasive manner, and, seeing me safely seated over my eggs and hominy, in equal good humor with them and with himself, he sallied forth to put my nag in readiness. My breakfast was soon discussed, and my horse at the door. My host, however, did not seem so willing to part with me. I had dropped the usual *quid* into his hands, saying good humoredly:

"There, plain Yannaker, we are quits for this time."

He laughed.

"You are a clever chap, and I somehow like you. We takes a liking for a human every now and then, jest the same as we takes for a fine horse, or a speaking hound; and I've got a notion that when you give yourself time you're a raal good fellow. Aint you?"

"There's more than you who think so," I answered with boy sharpness.

"Oh! git out," said he, "nobody beside yourself. But where away, lad? You're not a guine running after that gal you seed last night?"

"I am though," I answered doggedly.

"No, don't. Take an old fool's counsel for once, and save your horse's wind. In the first place you can't find her."

"I'll try for it."

"And in the next, if you do, it'll be much worse than shaking hands with a hungry bear that aint willing to be friendly at no time."

"Indeed ! But what know you of her? You told me you knew nothing."

"Well, in one way, that's true enough; and when you gets to be as old as me, you'll find out for yourself, that a gal child is about the hardest critter in the world to know entirely. But I wasn't speaking of any danger from her, by no means,—but of them that, mout-be, you'll find along with her."

"Ha! That old uncle of hers?"

"Prehaps,—and a rough colt, I tell you, to deal with, take him at any turn. Bud Halsey is all bone and gristle, I tell you, from tooth to toe-nail."

"Is his name Bud Halsey?"

"Yes, when he comes to Yannaker's,—but I can't answer for it any where else. All I can say is, that your course lies in any other part of the world than where he is. I say so, lad, for your good,—for, as I told you, I somehow likes you."

"But what is he, friend Yannaker?"

"He! He's nothing, as the world goes,—but something, I tell you, when he works his grinders. Keep clear of him, that's all. It don't become me to be talking behind the back of a man that pays his way in good money,— and I never axes such a man how he gets his money. That's no business of mine. But, to begin agin, and to end, lad, at the same time—keep clear of that gal's track;—it can't be that you've got so deep into the mire at one sight, so there's no reason to go deeper. Go home, and let Bud Halsey's niece marry some body else."

Yannaker was evidently no sentimentalist. His phraseology, which likened love to a bog, and the lady to a wild beast, or angry cur at least, seemed to me nothing to the purpose, and strangely savage and unpoetical. I answered him in a way intended to be conclusive, as I flung my leg over the saddle.

"Thank you, friend Yannaker,—you no doubt mean me kindly, but if Bud Halsey were twice the monster that he seems, I'd take his track."

"Well, it's cl'ar, lad, that you've been pretty much used to having your own way, and such people are never made wise, but by a little worry,—so go ahead, as quick as you please,—only keep your eyes busy, believe nothing that you hear, be scared at nothing that you see, and be ready to treat a man with two legs as if he was an animal with four;—for, if you go after Bud Halsey, there's no telling whether man or beast will sprawl first. If you must have the ways of a man, be sure you have the heart of one. There's no telling how many dangers a stout heart will carry a fellow through."

Something piqued with the tone of this discourse, I struck spurs into my steed, and sent him through the gateway, as I replied:—

"Thank you, thank you, friend Yannaker—I have no fears, so do you have none. I trust your eggs won't give out before I return. I shall be back by Christmas for my egg-nog."

"Go ahead!" was all of his response which reached my ears,—but I could hear him mutter something more, as, shading his eyes with his hands, he watched my progress along the road.

CHAPTER FOUR

My reader, if he still has in his veins any of the hot blood of his early man-hood, will easily understand how the exhortations and warnings of the landlord, so significant and forcible as they were, should have awakened in me the spirit of curiosity, and prompted into activity my natural passion for adventure. My damsel became, in my eyes, the heroine of romance, to be rescued from the bearded giant—to be won with feats of arms, and the most reckless audacity. I began, the moment I was fairly out of sight of Yannaker's, to examine the neat silver mounted pistols,—the property of a dear departed brother—which had long been my favorite possession, and which I now carried in the pockets of my overcoat. It will amuse, rather than alarm, the reader, to describe these mortal weapons. They were of the smallest calibre, capable of carrying only a buckshot, and useless for any purpose unless with their muzzles fixed upon the very bosom of an enemy. But I had little experience which could test their value. Like other boys, I had been taught by a tender mother that lead and powder were horridly dangerous things, and that pistols were pistols. As I gazed on the pretty playthings which I carried, and saw that the priming was dry and grainy, I was inspired with as much confidence in their efficiency as ever had that famous knight—I forget his name—who wielded *Excalibar*—in that spell-endowed weapon. A dirk-knife, of more respectable dimensions which I wore in my bosom, completed my equipments in this respect.

I need not say that I pursued my way almost at random. I have said that four roads diverged into different regions of country, from the area in which the house of Yannaker stood. I had dashed on that which had presented to the casual eye the most obvious carriage track, and with all the ardor and the hope of youth, I followed this route till sunset, when I found myself in front of a wigwam, in the door of which stood a haggard woman, scarce able to move, bearing in her countenance all the proofs of a severe visitation of autumn fever. From her I learned that no carriage had passed that day, and, indeed, before I made the inquiry, I had lost all fresh traces along the road of the vehicle, which I had set out to follow. Here was a quandary. To return then was out of the question. My love and romance together failed to inspire me with any desire for riding back over such a road, and on a night which promised to be equally cold and starless. To go farther was idle, considering my objects, and I gathered from the woman of the house that her dwelling was the only one on that road within fifteen miles. I was perforce compelled to remain where I was,—a necessity which, when I saw the cheerlessness of the interior, was felt to be even heavier than the protracted journey. But for my faithful horse, I had taken the back track, and seen 'plain Yannaker' by the next day's dawn.

I must hurry over the next three days. They were unmarked by any event of importance. Nothing had occurred having any bearing on my purpose, nor did I feel or find myself, up to this time, one step nigher to the fair object who was still the warmest and most vivid presence in my imagination. I had, meanwhile, retraced my course to Yannaker's, heard more of his warnings with as little heed, tried another of the roads diverging from his house with as little profit, and now, in a third direction, was laboring at the close of day among the swamps of Choctawhatchie. That night, the brown heath and dried leaves formed my bed, my canopy was the tree and sky, while a rousing fire at my feet, and in front of my horse, served to keep at a distance any beasts of prey which might have been disposed to disturb us. I confess I slept little. I had not so much faith in the effect of fire upon wolf and tiger. I was in a region where they still were found, and what with seeing to the comforts of my horse, gathering brands, and trying to keep warm, the morsels of sleep which I caught were equally small and unsatisfactory. It was more refreshing to me to get fresh glimpses of another day.

Once more afoot, and with the dawn. My brave steed had borne the privations of the night better than myself. At least he wore a more cheerful aspect in the morning—and this encouraged me. I dashed forward with that neck-or-nothing philosophy which feels itself prepared for whatever may turn up, though with a lively hope that it may take the shape of break-fast. No man can endure long the want of hunger as well as sleep. One or other he may stand with tolerable fortitude for thirty-six hours, chewing the cud of his reflection, in the absence of tenderer meats,—but denial of both, for such a period, will go nigh to unnerve and undo the bravest. Just then, however, I felt very sure there was no standing hunger half so long. The idea of a smoking breakfast, I modestly confess, had put to slumber, for the time, certain other far more sublimated ideas.

I had not to ride far—perhaps some eight miles—before I found my breakfast. This was at an Indian cabin, as miserable a mud hovel as ever engendered vermin, and reduced humanity, a willing victim, to their ravages. My host was a half-breed,—one of those dark, untamed, surly savages, such as the Indian, with a white cross, almost invariably becomes. He placed my food before me as if it was poison. His looks, indeed, seemed to defeat its alimentary properties, for I ate with suspicion, and it did little help to my digestion. Fortunately, my horse found no such fault with his corn and fodder, probably because he looked at them rather than the hands by which they were furnished. My host eyed me in silence, took my money with the air of one who would just as lief take my life, and watched my departure from his door with the indifference of one who is assured that it must be taken wherever I may go. My reflections, owing to sleeping in the woods, starvation, bad food, and sulky savages, had become far less audacious, knight-errantlike, and consolatory than usual. There was but one remedy for them, and that lay in the spur at my heels. I touched up the sides of my horse, whom a hearty breakfast had rendered somewhat dull, and on we went, dashing through a region that not only grew more wild, but more watery at every step. The conviction that a river was at hand, reminded me that my incognita had said that she lived beside one, and this memory, with the increased rapidity of my motion, served to disperse in some degree, my disquieting reflections.

It was towards midday, when I was suddenly startled by sounds, like those of a horse, at some little distance before me. This led me to prick up my senses a little, and feel in my pockets for my pistols.

But, just then, I had no need of them. A moment more shewed, and dissipated, the occasion of my alarm. Man and horse came suddenly in sight, wheeling out from a little Indian trail, a little ahead, and on the right hand of the path which I was pursuing. The horse was a miserable hack, driven to the top of his speed—which was no great matter,—by the unre-laxing application of whip and spur. The rider was evidently engaged in a race for life. He was a small person, well wrapped up in clothes, with a brand-new beaver on his crown, and a smart whip with an ivory handle in his grasp. His boots and unmentionables, originally of city make and good cloth, had been in close acquaintance with the tenacious yellow mire, which was abundant enough at every turning. His face was sharp and his eyes vigilant; at an ordinary time, and under ordinary circumstances, it is probable that their expression was sufficiently shrewd and sagacious, but just then, it was pale with fear, and expressive of no other quality. The man was evidently half-scared to death. I drew up and faced him. He would have dashed aside in consternation, regarding me as an enemy; but my voice arrested and somewhat quieted him. Besides, having unconsciously planted my heavier steed directly across the track, no spurring or whipping that he could use, could force forward the feeble animal he rode. He was accordingly, breathless and looking back, compelled to stop.

To make a long story short, he had been robbed, most civilly, according to his own account, some three hours before. His business had been to collect certain monies, in which object he had succeeded. The money —a considerable amount—had been promptly paid him by his debtor, from whom he had taken leave and gone upon his way rejoicing. But he rejoiced not long. An hour had not elapsed, ere he was accosted by the rogues, two in number, and they—women.

"Women!" I exclaimed with equal astonishment and mirth. The pitiful fellow shrunk beneath my glance, and made a stammering explanation which half excused him. According to his belief they were women only in costume. Like the worthy Welshman, in the case of Falstaff—*he* "liked not when a 'omans has a great peard; *he* spied a great peard under her muffler." One of the rogues, it seems, had been so indifferent to propriety of costume, as to make her toilet without shaving; and a grisly beard a month old, had made the pistols which she presented to the breast of the collector, doubly potent in his eyes. The pistols were clearly masculine. Having relieved him of his pleasant burden, they laid a hickory over his own and horse's back,—a mode of objurgation which horse and man seemed equally prepared to comprehend. He heard but the one comforting assurance that they gave him at parting, that if he only dared to look back for an instant, like Lot's wife, they'd salt him forever. He had ridden some fifteen miles since leaving them taking care to incur no such penalty. His farther information, was of some color for my own prospects. He gave it as his opinion, that the whole region, which he had fancied a *quasi* wilderness, was alive with rogues—that the settlement was quite a numerous one—that they occupied every fastness and place of cover, and retreat— hammocks and islets—in the swamps and river

> "And ever alley green,
> Dingle, or bushy dell, of this wild wood,
> And every bosky bourn from side to side."

They were a vast community, kept together by the common object and necessity, roving always in concert, and sworn against all laws and all honesty. He did not scruple to declare his conviction, though this he did in a whisper, and with an eye cast furtively around him, that even his debtor, who had paid up so promptly, was of the very same fraternity, who had only paid so readily because he well knew that his associates, would very soon put him again in possession of the same money.

"And who was your debtor?" I asked with some indifference, as a matter of course, and almost heedless of the answer.

"His name's Bush Halsey."

I felt my cheeks glow again. "*Bush* Halsey?—are you sure it is not *Bud* Halsey?"

"Oh, yes! He's got a brother named Bud Halsey."

"And where's he? Is he here in the swamps?"

"No, I guess not. I heard of him night afore last, down to'ther side of the 'nation,' but he's gone below."

"Gone below? where?"

"I can't guess."

"And how shall I find this Bush Halsey?"

The poor fellow was unwilling or unable to give me directions. His fright revived when he recollected some threats that were thrown out, of future treatment, if he dared to reveal anything in relation to the robbery, and my anxiety to get intelligence, and my determination to go forward, —expressed in spite of his counsel to the contrary—now seemed, all on a sudden, to impress him with the belief that I was one of the gang, and no better than I should be. An attempt which I made to get some further information touching the Halseys, only rendered him more anxious to shake off an acquaintance who might think proper, at some sudden moment, to finish those feminine proceedings which had been begun in the swamps; and, seeing his disquiet, I wheeled my horse out of his path, and bidding him God speed, boldly turned into the dark, narrow avenue out of which he had emerged.

CHAPTER FIVE

I was certainly about to pursue, with sufficient audacity, a career, which, with sufficient audacity, I had begun. The romance of the thing was still uppermost in my mind. The truth is, that youth, unaccustomed to trials of its own, is not always persuaded of the realness of danger. There is always a hazy indistinctness about the wild events of which it reads or hears, which, touched by the warm rays of an unrestrained imagination, becomes a glory in its sight, and effectually hides from view the cloud and storm from which it has arisen. I was moving forward as one in a dream. Accustomed to a life of security, and to the even progress of the day, unbroken by anything unusual, and secure from any evils which are not common every where to life, I could not and did not yield my belief to the strange stories which I heard. That they were commended to my fancy, was natural enough, as they came clothed with the hues of the picturesque and novel. But that they were real, actual, living and daily occurring things —that here, in America—in our matter of fact, monotonous, prosaic day,—there were bonafide brigands, such as we read of in Italy,—was a matter not so easy to be brought within the compass of belief. Thinking from my feelings, I judged the affair of the fellow with whom I had just parted, to have been some clever practical joke of some dare-devils, exaggerated by his unmanly terrors, and hereafter to be explained when the trick had been sufficiently played. Then the robbery had been committed by women. Only think of my being bid to stand by my own little incognita! The fancy made me laugh outright, and I felt very certain that, in such an event, I should take to her arms, with the full purpose of using my own. I did not actually wish to encounter her in the character of a footpad, but I felt that such an event would not be entirely without its pleasant accompaniments. A wrestle with her did not seem an affair to inspire terror; and, laughing at the conceit, I dashed forward, muttering from Dick, the apprentice,—

> "Limbs do your office and support me well,
> Bear me to her, then fail me if you can."

Filled with such pleasant musings, I had ridden probably three quarters of an hour, after parting with the Collector, and in this time I had overcome an interval of four miles—not more,—for the road, originally an Indian trail, was broken by numerous *bottoms,*—mucky places, of which the reader will form a sufficient idea from the distich written with coal, upon the blaze of a tree, which stood fronting a place of similar character, called *Cane Tructa,* through which I once had to pass:

> "Here's h——ll, and it
> To go through *yit.*"

The citizen would only need to gaze upon such a spot and acknowledge the same necessity, to feel the force and propriety of such an inscription. The poet was worthy of the subject, and that is no mean praise. I had gone through some three or four of these miry gulphs, which the most reverent nature would be very apt, involuntarily, to liken to the infernal regions, Acheron and Styx—though none of them was so bad as *Cane-Tructa,*—and had at length emerged upon a high and beautiful knoll of green, the sloping edges of which were fringed with dense barriers of cane, their feathery tops waving gently, like the plumes of so many gigantic warriors,—and was advancing, in an easy lope, into an area, about two hundred yards round, on which trees seemed never to have grown,—when my horse suddenly stopped short, and shyed half round, while his elevated head and ears attested some occasion of alarm. I raised my eyes, and discovered—directly on the path in front, squat upon a log, the butt end of which was thrust out from the opposite forest,—a man in a grey overcoat, with slouched hat, and a huge rifle which lay directly across his thighs. The suddenness of the encounter a little staggered me; but, remembering my fanciful philosophies, and the ludicrous plight of the Collector, I soon recovered myself, and determined promptly to yield myself to any mirthfulness which the mischievous nature of men, in such situations, might be disposed to practice. But as soon as I got nigh enough to notice the exact features of the man before me, I arrived at the conclusion, instinctively, that he was no *amateur.* He was one of those men, whom we know at a glance, as persons of downright, serious business,—who never laugh,—

who know nothing in life but its necessities,—and regard all things and all persons, with that hard-favoured earnestness, which looks directly and only to the most slavish calls, whether of a hunger that needs, or an appetite which lusts. He neither moved limb nor muscle as I approached, yet I could see that his eyes observed me keenly. The reader will be pleased to remember that I am of the sanguine temperament—a temperament which acts promptly, without much reflection, from a spontaneity, the result, it would seem, of a corresponding and equal activity of mind and feeling. The truth is, such persons *think* with as much rapidity as they move, and if rightly trained to habitually just thinking, their impulsive movements are very apt to be quite as correct in their tendencies as if they were made under the most deliberate exercise of thought and will. This is said to account for my conduct on the present occasion. It did not appear to me that I thought at all of what I should do. But the resolution and the performance were one. As I approached the stranger slowly, I threw my left leg over, so as to sit entirely upon the right, thus facing him fully as I drew nigh. This is a favorite mode in the Southern country of sitting a horse, when the rider meets with a friend, or with any one in whom he has confidence, or with whom he is disposed to linger and converse. It shows that there is no trepidation and no desire of flight. Sitting thus, I approached the fellow, and stopped my horse directly before him. He looked up at me with a savage sort of inquiry in his glance, as if to say "what next?" I did not suffer him, however, to put the question in words, but proceeded in the following manner:

"I have but one question, stranger, before I begin, and that is, 'am I safe here from a sheriff?' Be quick and tell me, for I must ride until I am."

"And what makes you afraid of a sheriff?"

"You're not one, I hope?"

"Rather guess not."

"Very well! Now then—do you ever see one here?"

"No! They take root here but never grow. A deputy came here once, from somewhere below; they planted him, but he never come up."

"Good! I need go no farther then;" said I, dropping from my horse, and taking a seat beside him on the log.

"Whar' are you from?" he asked.

"Tennessee."

"What's brought you here?"

"This!" said I, jerking my horse's bridle as I spoke. The fellow glowered upon me, with looks that showed he was no joker, as he responded—

"You mean to say you come on him?"

"Not exactly, though I did come on him. But the horse caused my coming here, I made a swap, giving that nag, which you see is a fine one, with a fellow at muster, who traded me a creature that had spavin. We didn't see it at first, for he was warmed with riding. But going off from muster I stopped at a friend's house, where I sat an hour. Meanwhile the horse had cooled off; and was as stiff in her joints as if they were made of ridge poles. I had got on a mile farther, hardly able to get along, when who should come by but Backus, the fellow I had swapped with. When I saw my own fine animal that he was riding, and felt that I could hardly hobble along with the one I rode, I got down and stopped him, jerked him from the beast, and we got to blows. Somehow he got a knife in him, and I got my horse back. People would have it 'twas my knife did the mischief, and there was an inquest, and a warrant—and all that sort of thing,—and so I sloped—but look you,—you're sure you're not a sheriff or a deputy?"

"And if I was?"

I grappled him by the throat in an instant, and drew my dirk, which flourished in his eyes before he could say "Jack Robinson!"

"Hold off, stranger!" he exclaimed, grasping my arm. "I'm no sheriff —and no deputy. D———n the breed,—I'm just as much afraid of 'em as you."

"Well you spoke in time!" I said, with a half subdued fierceness of look—"it's no time to play with a man when his neck's in a plough line."

It required no small effort, I assure you, to compose my muscles and carry on this game without laughter. But I felt that it was now necessary. If my neck was not absolutely in a halter, it was very clear to me that my life was not in a state of absolute security. One glance at the ruffian at my side, had served to dissipate all my romantic fancies.

CHAPTER SIX

Thus far I had carried out my assumed character, with tolerable success. I had certainly lied with a natural grace and readiness that did not need a prompter, and I had the satisfaction to see that my new comrade, in his own mind, took me to be as great a scoundrel as himself. I somewhat blushed for myself, as I became assured of this, but blushing then was no part of my policy. I was in for it, and had to go through. I remembered the counsel of old Yannaker at parting, and salved the hints of conscience by reflecting that I was in the rogues atmosphere. Every step I took with my companion left this matter less in doubt. Though by no means a garrulous fellow,—really, a fellow of few words, he contrived, in those few words, to give me insight into many and very strange things. Assuming that the circumstances under which I had sought refuge in the swamp, and my own inclination, had already made me one of the fraternity, he gave me a brief but comprehensive history, of their doings and ways of life. What had been told me by the Collector was fully confirmed. The region in which I wandered, was possessed by a community of rogues. They were numerous and extensively connected throughout the country. Some of them had absolute wealth; and children, born in this American Alsatia—so long had it been a realm of outlawry,—were now grown to manhood. What a history was here. I asked myself, while my cheek glowed again,—was my beautiful unknown, one of these? Had she drawn her infant breath among such scenes, such rogues—had such always been her connections,—and in what degree had she escaped the contaminating influence of such an atmosphere of crime. The robbery of the Collector, by persons in female garments, now struck me—as it did not when I first heard of it—with a sort of horror. I could feel the enormousness of the crime, committed by women, when I thought of *her*, as one, who might be in training for like practice. But when I thought of her more particularly—when I remembered that night—her shy and timid air—her subdued and gentle accents,—and the tenderness that spoke out equally in eye and voice,—I was re-assured. I felt happy in the conviction that no sort of human training, could pervert such an exquisite work of heaven.

Enough of this,—and let us hurry forward. We were on our way together into the recesses of the swamp. This was an admirable receptacle —a retreat, in which pursuit of one, familiar with the region, would be undertaken by a thousand men in vain. Pursuing a zigzag and continually changing course for several miles, I yet conjectured that we were not more than one mile from the spot where we started. A long dim avenue, led us as through some lonely corridor, into a spacious area, a chamber almost surrounded by water, opening only upon one defile, which might be guarded by a single man. Here and there were nooks, closets, as it were, of forest, which one might select for studio or dressing room, and be secure from passing interruption;—and anon, you had larger fields of operation —halls fit for courtly audience—vast parlors, of green wall and azure ceiling. But the reader must conceive for himself, what the rapidity of such a narrative as this, will not suffer me to describe. Enough, that love could not easily contrive such a labyrinthine bower, for the safety of the beloved one, with all the appliances of art at his bidding, and all the resources of imperial wealth at his command. Woodstock was a fool to the swamp city of Conelachita!

By little and little I made new discoveries. Here was art as well as nature. Sometimes little tents of bush would appear,—snug cottages for a single sleeper. Anon came a more permanent if not a more pleasing hovel, made of logs and clay. Here a horse would be seen fastened—his saddle and bridle hanging to the tree above him; now a face would peer out from the copse beyond us, as the trampling of our steeds would become audible; and now a whistle, or the bark of a dog, would announce our approach, to distant echos, which would be sure always to be on the watch, to take it up, and repeat the signal to others yet beyond. All this was so much romance, which made me half forgetful of the risks I incurred, and of the policy I was to pursue, in order to escape them.

At length, my conductor came to a halt. "Here," said he, "let us hitch —we must take boat here." I stopped, got down, and followed his example. We fastened our horses to swinging limbs, and set forward. I discovered that we were on a sort of islet, on the edge of a river—a dark, deep, but narrow stream, which whirled by us with the rapidity of a four knot current, carrying along with it reeds and branches, and sticks, the tribute of numerous shores, on the several creeks above. A neat little *dug-out,* capable of carrying two persons only was fastened at the landing. "You can paddle your hand I suppose?" said my conductor. Could I not? I could have paddled both hands. It was one of my favorite exercises from my earliest youth, on my own noble river, the Alabama. I answered him by taking my seat in the little bark, that danced like an egg-shell upon the whirling current. "She's a clean critter," said my companion with evident satisfaction. His praise was deserved. A better balanced canoe, of better proportions for such a stream, I had never beheld. It was a pleasure to send her forward, and we found no difficulty in crossing the river;—but, having made the opposite shore, we followed it up, until we passed into the mouth of a creek, a broad but sluggish stream. This we ascended for half a mile or more, when we drew up to some tolerably steep banks, jumped ashore, and hauled the canoe into a *crevasse,* which might have been the work of hands. We had not gone far when we heard a voice. The person did not appear, and the language used was a sort of gibberish beyond my comprehension. It seemed to be understood, however, by my companion, who turned aside at once, and entered upon another path. Here we met another person who regarded me attentively, but went forward without a word. The next moment we encountered two women, possibly the very feminine rogues who had robbed the Collector, but if they were, they had taken care to shave themselves since they shaved him,—for their chins,—and I examined them heedfully as they past—were quite as clean as his pockets. They did not pass in silence, however, but had a few words of common-place, and a nod and a smile to me. They were young too, the jades, but quite ugly enough to have frightened the Collector, without rendering necessary the show of pistols. A whistle, once, twice, thrice, repeated, at stated periods and places, now notified our approach to higher personages, and emerging from the avenue into an area, we came upon a group of five men, who seemed to be busy about a canoe of considerable dimensions, which was yet in the log, though the burning and hewing had been begun. One of them, who was stooping over the log, seemed to be engaged in describing the outlines. He rose from his stooping posture as we approached, and discovered to me a person not only of large frame, but of imposing presence. He was over six feet in height, broad breasted, sinewy and muscular, with limbs of admirable symmetry, which his costume, which was all of buckskin, made Indian fashion, showed off to great advantage. His coat was a hunting shirt thickly fringed; no longer fresh in its original bright yellow, but subdued by exposure to the weather, to an uniform *umberous* aspect. There was no covering on his head, the hair of which, though thick and long, was white as cotton. His beard, which spread over his bosom in thick curling folds and masses, was such that, if I had not felt sure that he was only a great rogue, would have led me to suppose that he was a great patriarch. His eyes were large, deeply set, and of a clear dark blue. His nose was Roman, his mouth small and expressive, and the whole expression of his face that of benignity, and a conscience quite at rest with his fellows and the world. I add that, as he wore neither stock nor neckcloth, there was scarcely anything in his costume or appearance, to remind me of civilized life, and yet, even with his habit borrowed from the Indian, there was quite as little of the savage. The picturesque in his guise, and its noble simplicity, according so happily with his features and his frame, effectually relieved his appearance of that which might otherwise, in my sight, have seemed strange and unnatural. He extended his hand at my approach, a slight change of expression from interest to civility, being apparent in his countenance, then, after giving some directions to the workmen, he drew aside with my late companion. A few moments only had elapsed when he returned, having, as it would seem, in that time, gathered from the latter all the knowledge which he had respecting me. He again gave me his hand, and drew me aside from the rest.

"You have been unfortunate, young man," said he,—"and I am sorry for you. There can be no greater misfortune than taking life, particularly at your age. But Fry tells me you had provocation. Pray, how was it?"

I had to begin anew the work of invention. Of course, my story, in substantial particulars, must be the same as I had told before. But there was a difference, which I soon discovered, between my present and former companion,—while, to the latter, I appeared reckless; to the former, as a man evidently better acquainted with human nature, I adopted another tone. He had himself indicated my cue, when he spoke of the provocation which I had received. He knew enough of the superior nature and education—which I felt that I could not, and did not wish to, conceal—to be aware that no such crime is ever committed by such in wantonness, or from the mere brutal instinct of passion. There must be provocation and hot blood, in the case of the educated man—with very few exceptions— before he will do murder. I framed my story accordingly. He heard me patiently, and I was particularly careful to say no more than was necessary. This is the great secret in lying successfully. When I had done, he took me kindly by the hand.

"Here you are safe," said he, "as long as you choose to remain. You know what we are, and must abide by our laws. We ask you for no participation in our practices, unless your own will inclines you that way,—which I would not encourage. This affair may blow over—your friends may succeed in hushing it up, and then you may return in safety to your family. Nay, even we may do something towards this result, however strange you may think it. Outlaws ourselves, we have friends not only among those who obey, but those who administer the laws. What is your name, and from what part of Tennessee do you come? Let me know those particulars, that we may institute an inquiry, and see what can be done for you at home."

Here was a dilemma. But there was no time for delay. It was necessary to answer promptly. I gave my name as Henry Colman, of Franklin County, West Tennessee. It was fortunate for me that I knew something, personally, of this region, for it appeared so did my examiner, and he subjected me to a keen scrutiny, in which I did not dare to falter. My answers seemed satisfactory. He pressed my hand, and bade me go along with him, and we rejoined the persons we had left.

To these I was not introduced, and he only remained with them long enough to give some directions on ordinary subjects. This done, he bade me go with him, and we pursued our way together through a long wood, occasionally crossing branch and creek, upon a rude log or fallen tree. My companion was free of speech, and his conversational resources, I soon found, were equally admirable and ample. He was deeply versed in books—he had seen the world, and was not insensible to its refinements. His eye was evidently one accustomed to seek out and discriminate the forms of beauty in external objects, and he frequently drew the regards of mine to this or that point of view in the surrounding landscape, which was either picturesque or fine. All this, while it increased my respect for him, lessened the impressions which I had received of his objects and associates. I found it more and more difficult, at every moment, to believe in his outlawry. It was all some pleasant jest—some queer contrivance of clever people, to produce a laugh at the expense of the credulous;—and with this notion, I was more than once provoked to blurt out the truth in my own case, and my convictions in theirs, in order to show that I was a little too sagacious to be fooled further than I thought proper. But a lurking grain of prudence, at the bottom of my brains, prevented me from so precipitate a proceeding. Besides, had I not an object—was not this Mr. Bush Halsey, and was not Mr. Bush the brother of Mr. Bud Halsey, and did not Mr. Bud Halsey have in charge my beauty of the cloud—my fair unknown—the dark-eyed, mysterious damsel of whom I was in search? But where was she and that grisly personage? Except in size, there was no resemblance between the supposed brothers. I confess that when I recollected the rude stare and deportment of the latter, I was in no great anxiety to meet with *him*—but my desire to see *her* rendered me comparatively indifferent even on this head. I was soon to be relieved on some of my doubts. We had now got into a region of upland swamp, which bore some of the marks of a more civilized settlement. A corn-field opened upon right and left, and cattle were lowing down the lane, wigwams appeared in sight, and a troop of barn-fowls were strutting to and fro in all the consciousness of corn and company. Beyond, might be seen a tolerable log-cabin, from which the cheerful smoke was arising, in a long spiral column, through the patriarchal branches of a clump of oaks.

"Here, sir, is our wigwam. A little rough, but not without its comforts. If we have not the laws among us, we are not without those things which the laws were intended to secure. Here, too, you will find a few books, and if you are a musician, there is flute and violin. I keep them, still, rather as proofs of what I have been, than what I am now—though the enjoyment of music is not absolutely inconsistent with the most desolate of human conditions."

I had observed, prior to this, that, on more than one occasion, the remarks of the senior had run into a melancholy tone; and I now discovered that there was a subdued expression in his countenance that looked like a settled sorrow. There was no unmanly whining, however, in what he said; but the incidental and unforced utterance of an habitual feeling, which, at such moments, was an appropriate echo to the thought which he had occasion to express. We entered the house together. It was the ordinary log hovel of the country. The room or Hall upon which we entered was a small snug apartment, fourteen by sixteen. Its chinks were all neatly covered with clapboards. Its tables were of common pine,—its chairs of domestic fabric also, seated with skins. Several tier of rude shelves on one side of the apartment contained the books of which he had spoken, which were certainly numerous for such a region. There, too, were flute and violin. The window—there was but one in the apartment,—was glazed and hung with calico, and my eye was fixed upon a slender rocking chair, which was cushioned with calico, and stood very near the fire-place. Such a chair could not have supported the huge frame of my host for ten minutes. By whom could it be occupied? I looked round and listened in vain. The dwelling had evidently no tenants but ourselves. Here was a disappointment. But, the rocking chair was a promise in which I put some faith, and there were other proofs of a female presence around us. There was a bandbox, speaking volumes of itself; and on one of the tables I discovered a little open basket full of squares of calico for quilting, and there was an unfinished stocking, with the bright needles sticking in it, peering out from a corner of the aforesaid basket,—and these were all signs of a feminine presence, which would not allow me to despair. But let us hurry through the day. Mr. Bush Halsey, for I soon discovered that it was he, indeed, treated me with the most marked attention. He played the country gentleman to perfection. A servant came at his summons, a neatly clad old African dame, who proceeded to set the table, and get us refreshments. At times, Mr. Halsey disappeared, leaving me to myself. And when he came in, it was always to renew some interesting conversation, and display his own proficiency in all its topics. I began to be very much pleased with the man, and, but for a natural anxiety which I felt, as to my situation and the result, which gave a little dullness and restraint to my manner,—I should have shown myself quite as happy and as much at home, as I had ever done at Leaside. That I was dull, Mr. Halsey ascribed to my feelings on the subject of the crime I had reported myself to have committed; and though he did not discourage such feelings, he addressed himself more than once to the task of strengthening me under them. His kindness was such that, even on his account, I half repented of the game I was playing. But I had not the courage to stop where I was. Indeed, there was no stopping. The cards, so far, were in my hands—but whether the prize deserved or, justified the venture, is a question to be solved hereafter. Day passed, the night waned, and my host showed me my apartment. For an hour after I had retired, I heard him playing upon the flute, and in such mournful caprices of sound as I never could have conceived before. It seemed to me that, if a heart could ever speak in music, such would have been the strains poured forth by a breaking one. This ceased, and I must have slept a little. I was certainly in a doze, when I was startled by an unusual noise. A door was grating, there was a bustle, the tread of several feet, then boxes or trunks were hauled over the floor, and there was a murmur of tongues,—subdued, as if to avoid unnecessary disturbance. This was followed by the opening of another door, and the voice of Mr. Halsey. "Ah! Helen. Is that you." Scarcely had he spoken, when other accents succeeded, which thrilled through my very soul.

"Yes, dear father. May I come in?"

"To be sure!" was the reply.

I could fancy the kiss and the embrace which followed. I could have sworn to that voice among a thousand. The bustle ceased, the sounds died away. There was no further stir that night. But my sleep was gone. Thought was too busy in my head for sleep; and with the first peep of dawn I was out of bed; but not sooner than my host. I saw him from my window, moving off towards the swamp, accompanied by the grisly guardian of my fair one. The tripping of light feet in the adjoining hall, drew my attention thither. Hurrying my toilet, I entered the apartment, and as I expected, discovered the object of my search. She sat in that very rocking-chair which had so much interested me the night before. Her back was to me, and she only half looked around as I opened the door. When she saw me she started to her feet with an exclamation of equal apprehension and surprise.

"Ah! you here!" she exclaimed. "Oh! wherefore have you come?"

"Did I not tell you that I could find you out—that I would follow?"

"Oh! why have you done so?" She spoke in manifest alarm, clasping her hands imploringly as she did so.

"And why not?"

"There is so much danger."

"I do not care for danger."

"But why risk it?"

"Because I love you."

"You love me?—oh, no! you must not. I am not for you to love. I am a poor girl of the woods. Go,—leave me soon. There is danger if you stay. You know not—you cannot guess the danger."

"No! There is no danger where you are."

"I!—I, myself, am danger," she exclaimed with a pretty energy. "The people will not love you here—go home to your own. Fly—leave us. You cannot go too soon."

"Your people shall be my people."

"It cannot be. You have your own father, your own mother."

"They shall be yours."

"No! no! My father is here!"

"He shall be mine!"

"Alas! you know not what you say. You know not me—you know not him. If you knew! If *you only knew!*" and she clasped her hands despairingly while she spoke.

"Nothing could make me love you less. I know *you*—that you are beautiful and very dear to me."

"Say not so! Leave me. Go your ways while there is yet time. Alas! I know not if it is not too late already."

"It *is* too late! I know where I am—among whom I am. Helen—I know all!"

"Alas! alas!"—She covered her face with her hands.

"But I would sooner be here with you, loving you as I do, than among the civillest people in the world. Only suffer me to love you—say that you do not hate me—that, were it with yourself, you would not have me leave you."

"Why should you think I could hate you."

"I do not think so."

"Do not—do not."

"Ah, Helen—could you grant me more. Could you but say that you would receive—return my love."

"I know not what it is to love."

" Let me teach you."

"No! no! you must go. I am a child—I must not listen and hear you talk such things. You do not, cannot know the truth—all the truth. Hear you, stranger—"

"Call me not stranger—call me friend—call me Henry Colman."

"Henry—is that your name?"

How sweetly did she speak the word! With what interest! I could almost have renounced my real name forever after that.

"Yes."

"Well, Henry, hear me, and believe me. There are bad men here, very bad men—they will do you hurt. Go home to your people while you can. You are not safe here."

"What! not with your father? He is good. He will protect me."

"Yes, *he* is good. He will do all that he can for you, Henry,—but he can not do all. My uncle is a fierce man—very violent—and it is not always that my father can keep him from doing wrong. Besides, Henry, my uncle likes you not. He saw you at Yannaker's."

"True,—but there's no reason why he should dislike me because he met me there."

"No!—but when he frowned, you frowned too;—and he didn't like that. He spoke of you. Oh! if he comes back and sees you here!"

"I shall not fear him, Helen."

"Beware of him—do not make him angry."

"Let him beware of me!"

"Hush! You know not what you say. He is the master here. He rules in the swamp. It is he who has brought my father here. Hark! They come. Oh! Henry, that you were gone—gone away—a thousand miles from this."

"You with me, Helen, and your prayer should be mine."

She cast upon me but one glance,—but that was sufficient. I felt, from that moment, that I was the master of her heart.

CHAPTER SEVEN

The moment after, her father and uncle entered the room. The latter looked at me with a keen, stern, searching glance.

"Who's this? Who have we here?"

He was answered by his brother.

"The young man, Colman, of whom I spoke to you."

"Colman! Colman! I have seen his face before."

It was the time for me to speak.

"You have, sir,—at all events, I have seen you. We met a few nights ago at one Yannaker's."

"Your memory is good, I see," was his reply, with something of a sneer in his accents. "But what brought you here? You followed us!"

"Scarcely, I think, else I should not have got here before you. My horse had very much the selection of the route to himself. In every respect he may be said to have brought me here."

"And who are you? What is your name?"

"My name is Colman—Henry Colman, sir. I am from West Tennessee. I have related to this gentleman all the facts in my history necessary to be known."

The tone of my speech was intended to show a proper degree of resentment at the abruptness of his, and to check the sort of cross-questioning to which he seemed disposed to subject me. His brother interposed.

"Yes, Bud, you have already heard."

"True,—but what of that. I have no objection to hear again. Truth never suffers from twice telling. I know the young fellow has killed his man about a horse, and flies here for shelter from the Sheriff. All very well, and very straight;—but what's the upshot of it. Does he expect to remain here forever—or does he propose at some convenient day to return, and blab every thing that he has seen and heard among those who give him protection."

"As a man of honor,"—I began.

He interrupted me.

"Hark ye, lad, were you a spy upon us, you would still insist, if questioned, that you are a man of honor. Perhaps, it is not men of honor that we want,—but bondsmen. We deal with our men as the devil is said to deal with them. We take security for their good will to us, by requiring of them the performance of some evil deed to others. Will you commit another crime? You see I do not mince the matter. Will you join us?"

I gave a single glance at Helen Halsey. I shall never forget the appealing expression of her dark and dewy eyes. Her hands were clasped—her form bent forward, as if waiting for my answer. That was tolerably prompt.

"What if I say 'No'?"

"Ha! You dare then?" and his brow grew black; the heavy muscles corrugating in little knots above his eyes, like so many young serpents coiled together, while his feet advanced, and his shoulders seemed to work convulsively, as if preparing for a mighty struggle. I receded a step, and put my hand into my bosom, as I replied:—

"I will not be driven by any man."

"Here, Bush Halsey, Helen's father, interposed, and drew the other aside. His words, which were those of entreaty and expostulation, only reached my ears in part;—but the reply of the other was fierce and loud.

"You are a fool, Bush, for your pains, and I am a greater fool for submitting to you, as I do. You should not meddle in these matters at all. You have nothing to do with them."

Here some words escaped me. Bush Halsey again spoke, and his reply was entirely lost. He spoke for several minutes, interrupted now and then only by some single expletive, uttered sometimes in scorn, sometimes in impatience, by the lips of the other. The final speech of the latter, set me at rest for the moment.

"Have it as you please. But let him not leave your own premises. If I find him prowling where he should not be, let him beware."

This was intended for my ears, for the glance which accompanied the words, was bestowed wholly upon myself. This said, he took one step towards us, then, suddenly wheeling about, without a farther syllable to any, he strode from the apartment. A moment before, and Helen had retired to her room. Her father then approached me.

"You hear the terms of your stay among us. It makes your retreat a prison, yct that is favorable to your circumstances. No reproach can be urged against you, for remaining where you are under a sort of duress. For your sake, I am glad that it is so. My brother is a violent man. We differ, as you may see, materially in temper. He has been rendered more violent, and perhaps unjust, by frequent injustice. Indeed, we have both suffered from a like cause; but it is my fortune still to remain somewhat human— possibly, because I have been left one human blessing which was denied to him. I am still a father. But come. Walk with me now, and I will show you your prison limits. You must not suppose yourself without privileges. Your bounds are not too close for sport and moderate exercise. The island which I occupy is free to you in every quarter, and it is not so small as you might imagine. Come, I will show you my dominions."

Our ramble was a long but pleasant one. My prison was a spacious one, well wooded and watered, completely insulated by creeks, and admirably chosen for the residence of a recluse. My companion carried me to his favorite walks—pointed out his fishing traps—his choice fishing grounds in spring and summer—a delectable bathing place, and more than one ample area, in which could be seen the implements of exercise, the quoit, the bar, &c., all convenient, and all arranged with the eye of experience and art. At certain points of view, I could see men on the opposite side of the creek, engaged in various duties, some sawing or chopping, others busy about boats and other matters, and now and then, one might be seen peering through a copse, as if engaged in no better business than that of seeing what his neighbors were after. The redoubtable Bud Halsey was no where visible. After all, my prison limits were not without their attractions. Every moment with Bush Halsey, proved him to be more and more a man of thought and observation. He was full of anecdote, sometimes indulged in a little bit of broad humor, and was at all times the most interesting companion. And when I thought of Helen, I smiled at the thought which could suppose that I could feel any privation, in the same prison bonds with her.

CHAPTER EIGHT

I pass over the events of a week—a period in which I suffered no annoyance, not even seeing for a moment the person of Bud Halsey. No doubt he was busy at his usual operations. His absence gave me no concern. Never was man happier than myself. Never did time pass so pleasantly. I began to love my venerable host, as well as his daughter. He certainly showed himself a most excellent man. Thoughtful, tasteful, philosophical, his nightly conversations were a rich treat that sometimes made me forget that Helen was by my side. Then, he had a most exquisite skill in music. His flute, after I retired at night, seemed the voice of some complaining angel. It was so mellow, so wild, so sweet and spiritually sad. Sometimes, at evening, when Helen would be absent, he would give me glimpses of his life, and the causes of his present situation. So far as I could gather from him, his worst crime was bankruptcy. He owed money which he could not pay. His person was threatened, and, with a morbidly keen sense of freedom, that shrunk from the idea of a goal as from degradation, he fled to the uncultivated forests—still in possession of the heathen—seeking safety. His child, meanwhile, remained with an aged relative. His brother followed him, but with less innocent conscience. His hands were stained with blood. He had incurred, without hope or excuse, the doom of outlawry—outlawry or death! But, on this subject, Bush Halsey said but little. That he should remain where he was, and in contact with a brother, whose deeds he certainly ventured to disapprove, is only to be accounted for by assuming for him a certain degree of phlegmatic irresoluteness of character. His temperament possessed nothing of the energy which distinguished that of his brother. He was mild, playful and persuasive; the other harsh, impetuous and commanding. I need not add that, save by his presence, he had no participation in the doings of the banditti in the midst of whom he dwelt. If the father improved upon acquaintance, how much more did the daughter. She was, indeed a wondrous treasure of the wilderness—not simply beautiful, but sagacious beyond her years and sex,—disguising, under the harmlessness of the dove, the wisdom of the serpent—under the simplicity of the child, the forethought and mature mind—on all subjects not conventional—of the high souled, intellectual woman. In merely worldly matters, she was a child. She had no conceal-ments. The thought spoke out in her eloquent eye, ere her lips could utter it—the feeling glowed, with a speech of its own, upon her cheeks, ere yet her mind could embody its character in thought. How soon did she show me that I had won her heart, and how confidingly, then, did she walk with me, speak with me,—let her fancy have its utterance, though every syllable and look betrayed her soul's dependence on my own. We rambled and we read together—she sang and I listened—as if we were both of the same household. We made every foot of our island limits our own. She knew the restraints set upon my footsteps, and when, in the delight of my heart, and the buoyant impulses of my spirit, I would have launched into the canoe, or borne her across the tree that spanned the creek, and conducted to the opposite territory, she caught my hand and restrained me.

"Do you think I fear, Helen?"

"But for my sake, Henry."

For her sake, it seemed to me, as if I could have done or forborne anything.

Thus we lived, and loved—need I say how happily and with how few qualifications. Yet qualifications there were. How was this to end? The ques-tion forced upon me a sort of self-examination, which, as it never resulted in my own acquittal, I never allowed it to be a protracted one. My conscience smote me for the game I was playing with this dear young crea-ture. I really had no purposes. It seemed as if I could have lived with her, and her only, all my life; but the idea of living all my life in that swamp retreat was unendurable. And to carry home with me as my bride, the daughter of an outlaw,—or, at all events, the niece of one,—was not to be thought of. I had lived too long in the world of convention not to have acquired certain laws and lessons which were fatal to the philosophies of anything so purely unsophisticated as Helen Halsey. Her heart was mine, but not her philosophies. Yet, truth to speak, I meditated no evil. I did not meditate this matter at all. Life was simply passing away in a delightful dream, and I was too much the boy to be willing to disturb its pleasant progress before the necessary time. But there were other qualifications to my enjoyment besides my own reflections. I discovered that my steps were closely watched. On the occasion when I first made this discovery, I had been standing with Helen on the bluff of a creek, admiring the proportions of as lovely a cockle-shell of a canoe as ever danced over Indian water. I had been trying to tempt her to enter with me. She had resisted and dissuaded me, and while we were discussing the project, my eye had suddenly caught the glimpse of a living object directly before me, on the opposite side of the creek. In that quarter the copse was exceedingly dense. Canes and water-grasses grew down to the very lips of the stream, and in the rear was a thick hedge of evergreens, shrubs and brambles, slightly sprinkled by heavy timber. A second look betrayed to me a pair of eyes keenly fixed upon our movements. In a moment they had disappeared. I quickly conceived the necessity of saying nothing on the subject of my discovery, and showing nothing in my deportment which could make it apparent to the spy himself. But the circumstance left me less at ease than formerly. Another day, within the same week, turning suddenly a little lane, with Helen, we passed three men, who observed us very closely. One of these men, particularly, struck me as one whom I had seen before, and the manner in which he eyed me, disquieted me, as tending to show that he too was striving in the work of recognition. But he passed on, and, with so many objects to divert and interest my thoughts, it was not likely that this should linger very long in my memory. I am very sure it would not have done so, but for other events of like nature, which kept the recollection fresh.

Meanwhile, where was Bud Halsey—that formidable and fierce bandit! I had seen nothing of him since that parting which had been so nearly a *meeting*. I was not sorry at his absence, and Helen shared my feelings.

"I'm so glad," said she, one day, as we loitered through as close a copse as ever favored the wishes of two foolish hearts;—"I'm so glad Uncle Bud is gone. Some how, Henry, I tremble when I think of him, on your account. You have defied him, and he don't like you."

"Nay, he can scarce be offended with me because I showed a proper manliness. Besides, what care we? So long as I do not pass the boundaries, there can be no chance of our quarreling, and I'm sure, Helen, unless you go with me, I do not care how long I remain in them. I could remain here for ever."

"Ah! you say so, but—"

"Truth, Helen. Have I not told you—how often—how much I love you? But you, Helen, have not spoken once. Will you not tell me, dearest, that you love me, too?"

"Oh! no! I do not feel as if I could say the word."

"But you feel it, Helen?"

"Oh! yes,—I feel as you could wish me;" and she turned and threw herself into my arms, burying her face upon my breast, and weeping unrestrainedly. Reader, were you a boy once?—have you a heart?—did you ever love? If yea to these,—you understand what I cannot describe—that moment of happiness! Until then I had regarded that verse in which Coleridge speaks of a similar event, as an exaggeration. In my silly conceits of convention—living among artificial men and women—I had thought it wholly out of reason, and all natural laws, that an innocent girl should be so audacious. But that scene convinced me—I could neither doubt the love, the truth, or the innocence of that dear child of the wilderness, and sweet and sacred to me now are those nature-prompted lines of the Bard of Genevieve:—

> "Her bosom heaved—she stept aside,
> As conscious of my look she stept,—
> Then suddenly, with timorous eye,
> She fled to me and wept.
>
> She half enclosed me with her arms,
> She pressed me with a meek embrace,
> And bending back her head, looked up,
> And gazed upon my face.
>
> 'Twas partly love, and partly fear,
> And partly 'twas a bashful art,
> That I might *rather feel than see*
> The swelling of her heart."

And thus we stood, thus we clung to each other, forgetting earth, almost forgetting heaven,—if such forgetfulness were possible, at a moment when we were in the enjoyment of that bliss, most like heavenly, the dearest known to earth—the full, precious acknowledgment, in the heart that we seek, of that passion which is flaming triumphant in our own!

CHAPTER NINE

How long we remained thus, for how many moments she clung thus passionately to my bosom, I cannot tell. The sense of enjoyment seemed to blind and render obtuse all the ordinary senses. I saw nothing, heard nothing, felt nothing, was conscious of nothing, but her sobs, her glistening eyes, upturned and seeming to melt in the intense gaze of my own, and that beating heart, which seemed bursting to yield itself to the custody of mine. In that moment we were torn asunder. A strong grasp was laid upon my shoulder, and I was hurled to the ground, half stunned, with a heavy knee upon my breast. In the same instant, the savage tones of Bud Halsey told me but too truly whence came the assault. It was under him I lay, with two of his myrmidons at hand, busy in preparing the ropes which were to bind me. Recovering from her first terror and surprise, Helen clung to his arms, imploring my release. But he repulsed her with rude hands and bitter accents.

"Away, you are bold, wanton—do you not blush—do you not hang your head in shame? Have not my own eyes surprised you in the embrace of this traitor?"

"Traitor!" was my exclamation.

"Ay, traitor—traitor and liar! We have discovered you. You are found out."

I did not speak. I struggled, but I need not say how fruitlessly. I was in the arms of a giant, and while he held me firmly, his two assistants passed their lines about my wrists, securing my arms behind my back. I was then permitted to rise.

"There," said my enemy, with a bitter laughter—"there, Helen Halsey, behold your lover. Oh! shame—shame upon you, Helen! What will your father say?"

"My father! He is here!" she exclaimed, with an accent in which delight and suffering seemed equally expressed. "Oh, father! how glad I am that you are come. Save him! Do not let them hurt him—he is innocent!"

It was at this opportune moment that the father made his appearance. She darted forward as she beheld him, caught his arm and drew him forward. His countenance was marked by doubt and inquiry, and was grave to sternness. He gave me but a single glance.

"Bud Halsey! what is this? Why have you bound the youth?"

"The serpent! You have been harboring a serpent in your bosom."

"What mean you?"

"'Tis as I thought. This fellow is a traitor—a spy upon us. He shall die the death of one."

"Oh, no! no! He is no spy—no traitor."

Such was the exclamation of the maid. The uncle turned upon her like a hyena.

"As for you, Miss, you should be silent for shame. Send her away, Bush Halsey—she has no business here. I found her in the arms of this fellow— close hugged—lip to lip! Ha! did I not?"

"Helen!" exclaimed the father.

"The girl's face was covered with her hands—her head drooped—she seemed ready to sink into the earth.

"Go home, Helen!"

She looked up timidly.

"Oh, father, you will save him? He is no traitor! He is innocent!"

"Are *you?*" he demanded in freezing accents.

"Oh! my father!" she cried in tones of mingled agony and reproach, as she threw herself upon his breast, and hid her face in his bosom. For a moment he seemed to press her there, then suddenly pushing her from him, uttered sternly but the single word—"Home!"

She receded from him, looked at me with a glance of deepest apprehension, then clasping her hands, as if in prayer, moved slowly out of sight.

CHAPTER TEN

When she had disappeared the father spoke.

"Now, Bud Halsey, what is all this?"

"It seems to me plain enough. Have I not told you? This fellow is a spy upon us—a traitor. He has lied—his whole story is a lie!"

The old man looked at me with stern but sorrowful glance.

"It is false! I am no traitor." I had uttered this assurance before—had spoken several times, particularly when the rude assault was made upon Helen by her brutal uncle;—but, in my excitement, though I very well heard and understood what was said by everybody else, I knew not well what I said myself. My asseveration now seemed to have very little effect,—upon Bud Halsey at least.

"Oh, my good fellow, we expect your denials. We look for no admissions from you,—no truth, as long as a lie will serve your purposes."

"A lie!" I exclaimed writhing furiously in my ropes.

"Ay, a lie! Look not so indignant at the charge, my lad,—we have made the discovery, that a lie comes easy to you. Your invention is good. But you will pay for it. You hang, by all that's powerful, to-morrow morning!"

"Hang!" said Bush Halsey.

"Even so!"

"Pshaw, Bud!—you cannot mean it. You are not serious?"

"As a judge! as a judge—the supreme judge, without appeal in all this region,—I have doomed him. He dies by sunrise."

The affair was looking serious. The ruffian continued,—interrupting the expostulations of his brother.

"The long and short of the matter is this. I have discovered that this lad, for his own purposes, has come among us with a lie in his mouth. Suspecting him at first, I dispatched Monks to Tennessee, to make inquiry as to the truth of the story which he told us. He has been all through Franklin County, and finds that the Sheriff has no process against any person named Henry Coleman, that nobody of the name of Backus has been murdered there, and the whole affair is a mere invention of this chap to find his way among us. Now what can be his object but treachery. He is a creature of the Sheriff. He would betray us. Well! he probably understands the conditions of his venture. He must abide them. You know our laws. He too shall know them."

"I cannot think the youth an enemy, Bud Halsey,—and you recollect he is my guest."

"And you are mine. You have no right to harbor a spy. Our safety makes this necessary. As for his being no enemy, that is possible, but I think him otherwise. Besides, as your guest, he has proved himself unworthy of trust, since he seeks the first opportunity to dishonor your daughter."

"You are a foul-mouthed liar!"—I exclaimed, "I love Helen Halsey. Never was mortal love less free from taint than mine. This, indeed, brought me here. I met her for the first time at Yannaker's—was pleased with her, and set out to find her. Circumstances helped me in the pursuit, and prompted the story which I told. It is true I am no murderer—no outlaw. But motive beyond what I have told you, I had none. Nothing but an honorable passion has prompted me in what I have done. This alone has brought me here.

"An honorable passion prompt a lie!" said the outlaw, with a sneer. "But," he resumed, "if this be true, you are ready to marry Helen Halsey?"

His keen eye seemed bent to search me through. The eye of the father also seemed on a sudden to watch me with a new interest. At that moment the idea struck me that the whole affair was a piece practice—a conspiracy among them—to force me into marriage; and, with this conjecture, indignant that I should be thus hampered, and forced into an engagement of the sort, I forgot the claims of poor Helen—nay, connected her with the scheme—suppressed my own strong yearnings for the prize thus proffered me, and replied doggedly:—

"I would not be compelled to marry an angel."

"Nor shall my child be forced on any one, Bud Halsey."

"Pshaw, Bush, you are a child yourself. How know you, man, that the measure is not necessary for her safety. Ay—look not so black and scowling—do you not suppose I feel like yourself?—but I say it again— to save her—to save her from shame!"

The frame of the old man was violently agitated. His lips were blanched to perfect whiteness;—for an instant his eyes glared on me with an expression akin to that tiger-look which his brother habitually wore,—and he exclaimed:—

"Speak not of this to me, Bud Halsey. I will not hear it even from your lips. Could I think it true, I should do murder myself. But it is not true—it cannot be true. Helen is as pure as any angel!"

"She is!" I exclaimed, fervently.

"Very well! I am glad to hear it—I am willing to believe it. You surely cannot be unwilling to marry an angel?"

The old man interrupted the outlaw.

"I tell you, Bud Halsey, that my child must not be named again in this business."

"And I tell you, Bush Halsey, that unless this traitor weds with Helen Halsey by sunrise to-morrow, he sees the last sunrise of his life. He dies an hour after. Take him away, men, and keep him safe in the new den!"

CHAPTER ELEVEN

I was seized by a couple of stout ruffians, who lifted me, head and feet, as if I had been a mere sack of straw, and hustled off upon their shoulders to the edge of the creek where a boat lay, into which I was tumbled with as little remorse as was shewn to Fallstaff when they emptied him out of the wick-basket into the Thames. They pulled down with me something like a mile, then landed on a sort of island, which seemed to be covered with an almost impervious forest. Once more lifted upon their shoulders, I was borne through narrow avenues of the wood a distance of some three hundred yards or more. Our course seemed to be a winding one. We at length reached a very strong log-house, consisting of a single apartment, probably twelve feet square. The logs were hewn and fitted closely. They were of the heaviest kind. There was no window, and but a single, and that a very low door, into which I was thrust headlong. Here I was left—the door fastened behind me, in a darkness that was rather increased than relieved, by an occasional gleam of sunshine that stole here and there through chink or crevice—to brood over my condition, and reconcile myself to the future prospect with what philosophy I could command. That prospect was no ways encouraging, and my philosophy was not of the most composing or consoling nature. I confess it, boy-like, I fell into very ridiculous and childish furies, the recollection of which, to this day, brings the blush into my face. I raved, and swore, and flung myself about upon the damp earth until I was tired. A few hours brought me to my senses. Darkness and silence are great subduers of passion—great promoters of reflection. Why will not our legislators discover this, and substitute imprisonment for life in place of that code, equally barbarous and ineffective, which violently tears away the sacred life principle, from the temple, made after the image of God, in which he has enshrined it? In the

darkness of the scene—a gloom, thick and seemingly solid and tangible—
which was spread around me,—and that awful stillness which seemed to
breathe in slumbers of the grave—I began to recover my half-banished
senses. I began to consider my situation. What was that? What was I to do?
What was my hope? It was now clear to me that, in spite of the kindness of
Bush Halsey's nature, he was powerless to save me. He himself lived but
upon terms with his outlawed brother, who, I was now persuaded, was as
reckless in his ferocity as he was unscrupulous in all moral performances.
That Bush Halsey would try, as he had already tried, to save me, I had no
question, even though he might have entertained some of the loathsome
suspicions which his brother had tried to thrust into his mind. But I had
marked too well the natural and enforced expression of defiance which the
outlaw had shown towards himself, not to feel very sure that there was no
hope from his interposition. And, as for the sweet, suffering Helen! She
would pray, I knew—she would be sleepless in the toil in my behalf;—
but what would it avail? I had already seen, in her frequent deportment,
how much fear she entertained of her brutal uncle, and though she might
acquire greater courage in approaching him than usual, having my danger
in view, yet, I could not deceive myself into the notion that much good
would result from any of her entreaties. Well,—the substance of my reflections led me only to this. I was in the meshes in a den of thieves and
murderers, doomed to death, and hoping nothing either from their mercy,
or their dread of legal vengeance. But there was one alternative,—one
outlet—allotted me of escape—to wed with Helen Halsey! Well, could I
stickle to avail myself of this alternative? Nay, was not this my own desire
but five hours before? Would I not have esteemed such a prize, a treasure
beyond all price, but a little while ago—the sole, great object of my desire?
Strange, indeed, what perverse mortals we are. My pride revolted at the
idea of being forced into possession of that which I desired beyond all
other objects. I now persuaded myself that uncle and father, were both in
a scheme to force me into these nuptials—that it was a cunning device to
restore to society some of her outcasts—one of those petty, dirty little
tricks of a base and cunning nature, of which I was to be the victim. I need
not say with what loathing I revolted at this suggestion—how indignant it
made me to think, that they could fancy me so dastardly, or so blind—
and I resolved rather to meet my fate, than dishonor my father's family,
by connecting myself with such a brood. Let me do myself justice, however. I never for a moment suspected Helen of any consciousness of this
design. No—I *felt* that she was pure and true. I did not think it. My heart

prevented my thoughts in her case, and, every feeling within me rose in arms against the slightest suggestion of my reason to this effect. Her heart had been pressed against my own—her face, covered with mingling tears and blushes, had been buried in my bosom, and that sacred pressure had been enough, not only to endear her to me forever, but to make me confident in her truth and loyalty. Ah! that first press of heart to heart, when both hearts are young and ardent. What a volume does it teach! What a life does it embody!—how full of assurances and inquiries, and promises and hopes,—sweet regrets,—and pleasures, so acute, as almost to be akin to pain! That first kiss of love—that first dear, stolen embrace,—the keenest joy of life, to which none after bears likeness,—in comparison with which all other joys are dwarfed! Still, quivering in my whole soul with the rapture of this embrace, I could not think of the dear girl, with whom I shared it, but as a victim like myself. Yet, so thinking, I would not stomach the necessity of being forced to wed her, by the imperious will of a person I despised. The more I brooded on this threatened necessity, the more I revolted from it, and resolved against it. 'No!' I exclaimed bitterly, in all the heroics of boyhood,—'sooner let me perish!'

Having reached this conclusion, I found composure. I stretched myself at length upon the ground, which I had now leisure to see was strewed pretty thickly with dried leaves, and was surprised by sleep;—and, dreaming of a fierce and deadly struggle with the outlaw, Bud Halsey, I was awakened, somewhere about midnight, by a rough hand laid upon my shoulder,—a rough voice, which I too well remembered, in my ears—and, flashing in my eyes, a huge torch, by the blaze of which I was half stupified and blinded. The intruder was Bud Halsey. He stuck the torch in a crevice of the wall, and calmly seating himself before me, regarded me with a glance of the keenest inquiry. I need not say that I returned it with one of scorn and defiance, and we looked upon one another in this manner, in a silence which lasted for several minutes. At length, he said:

"You do not seem to understand your true condition, young man. Did you suppose that I was trifling with you when I sent you here?"

"If you were," I answered, "it is a sort of trifling which I should be very loth to forgive, should the moment ever arrive when resentment would be to any purpose. I cannot suppose you were trifling."

"You are a lad of more sense than I had given you credit for. The rest ought to be easy. You see your condition. You have heard your fate. You have had time for reflection. Are you prepared? Will you choose? Will you hang, or marry the foolish girl you have dishonored?"

"You dishonor her by your foul breath, and foul imagination. She is pure as heaven."

"Pshaw! young man! Do you suppose me as unread as yourself in the history of human nature? Do I not know the weakness of woman's nature, and the recklessness of man's nature, when occasion serves and opportunity invites? But this as it may. I give you an alternative. If you have not wronged Helen Halsey, and you love her, as you profess, so much the less should be your reluctance to marry her. If you did not design to marry her before, as I suppose from your unwillingness now, there is every reason for suspecting you as I do, and taking for granted all the worst that one evil nature can imagine of another. On this subject we need waste no words. The simple question is before you. Will you marry her?"

"Where is her father? I would see and speak with him."

"You cannot."

"Why not? He will not refuse me."

"But I will! Look you, young man, Bush Halsey is, in some respects, as great a simpleton as yourself. If he had a voice in the matter, he would send you home to your mother, perhaps fill your pockets with gingerbread, pat you on the head, bid you go on your way rejoicing, and shed a flood of benevolent tears at your departure. But I am the master here! I am the outlaw! I do and counsel the robberies, and, if you please, I command and execute the murders. You know enough to make the task of confession on my part a very easy one. You know too much!—And this is the true reason of your predicament. You came here of your own free will, knowing among whom you came, and practising deception and falsehood to wind yourself in among our secrets. You are a spy, and our situation is such as to render us rather unscrupulous with that sort of persons. But I am willing to please my brother, and to gratify my niece. They are pleased with you, and I have not scrupled to say, and I repeat, notwithstanding your denials, that I think it necessary that you should marry her. It is for this reason that I propose to you this alternative, grant you this time for reflection, and seek you out at midnight to enlighten you more fully on the necessity of the thing. Had it not been for this, I should have had you knocked on the head without a word of parley; and, sure, that we should have no further trouble at your hands, should be now comfortably asleep, instead of sitting here, at midnight, endeavoring to make you sensible of your danger. There now—you have the whole, and what is your answer?"

The whole manner of the outlaw was so contemptuous, his tones so cold and sneering, his suggestions so unfeeling, and everything about him so offensive to my feelings, that I forgot my own danger, and replied promptly:—

"Nothing! I have no answer."

"Nothing! You have no answer?"

"None for *you.*"

"Very good! I leave you! You may look for me at sunrise, when you may probably be better able to find an answer. Good night."

Coolly detaching the torch from the wall, he waved it around so as to take in at a glance the entire apartment, and without further word, left the dungeon. The door was carefully fastened behind him, and the sound of voices without, led me to the conclusion that he did not omit the precaution of placing a guard upon the premises. In a few moments more I was left in darkness, and to my own reflections. These were not so gloomy. They were of a stern and angry sort. I had been irritated, not subdued, and, to confess a truth, I could not bring myself to believe that the case was so desperate as the outlaw made it appear. I could not think that Bush Halsey was so powerless, or that I should be abandoned to such a cruel fate. It was all a contrivance to terrify me into certain measures, and it was only a test of manliness which was to hold out longest. I was resolved not to show the white feather, and, after a while, fell asleep, as if nothing threatened in the morning.

CHAPTER TWELVE

"No! No!" I exclaimed at waking, which I did early,—"my neck was never made for a halter." I tried to raise my hands to it as if to assure myself that there was not one already around it, but the ropes with which I had been bound, and which, for the moment, I had forgotten, checked somewhat the exulting nature of my thoughts, as they checked the movements of my arms. I had been dreaming of the events which had taken place, and my exclamation was probably due to the character of my dreaming thoughts. I now repeated it, as if to assure myself, but it called up as unpleasant and unnatural an echo, as ever was heard in Killarney. The voice of Bud Halsey, speaking outside, replied:

"That's a matter about which no man is sure for thirty minutes. In fifteen, a cord may be adjusted, and where the woods are convenient, the affair may be all over in twenty. In your case, it still depends upon yourself whether you escape the present danger. You have still a few minutes to sunrise!"

The suddenness of the response, its character, and the character of the man by whom it was spoken, all combined to send a chill through my body, which it had not felt before. The next moment the door opened, and he appeared before me. You have already had a description of the man, but now there was a sly grin upon his features which they did not usually wear, and which seemed to betray a sort of satisfaction which he yet labored to discourage and keep down. The effort of a man passionate by nature, to subdue the show of impulses which are yet grateful, will usually result in some such conflict upon the features, than which, perhaps, there is nothing more unpleasant to behold. I had much rather seen him furious.

"Well, young man," he said, entering, "the time is at hand for your final answer. You have till sunrise. It will not be ten minutes before you see his red streaks on the top of that pine. Bring him out, men, that he may see more easily."

His orders were obeyed, and I found myself, still bound hand and foot, laid down before the door of the dungeon which I had just occupied. I now felt the cold, which I had not experienced to any very unpleasant degree during the night. But now I was chilled and uncomfortable, and what with the rigid position in which my limbs were fixed, and the effect of the keen morning breeze upon me, coming out suddenly as I did from one of the closest log houses, my teeth almost chattered. I fancied that the outlaw perceived my discomfort, and that he probably ascribed it to another cause, for his features put on that same expression of a satisfaction, which he yet labored to conceal. It was with some effort of will, that I succeeded in keeping down my tremors. There were some four persons, stout ruffians, loitering about. One was busy in building a fire, two others stood apart at some little distance, conversing in low tones together and looking occasionally at me, while, directly at my side, sat a fourth, coolly disentangling a ploughline, the probable uses of which I did not venture to conjecture. But it did not help much to lessen my shivering tendency.

"Step back a moment, Warner," said the outlaw to this assistant. "The lad has little time for talk."

The fellow did as he was bidden. He looked upon me as he moved away, and I fancied that I knew his features. I had seen him gazing at me once before, while I walked with Helen, and it then seemed to me that I had seen him elsewhere. I was now sure of it,—but where? At all events, if he ever knew me before, there was every reason to apprehend that he also would remember me. But I had not time to think of him. When he had withdrawn, Bud Halsey began, as he always did, with sufficient abruptness.

"Well, young man! the time is at hand for your final answer. You many not know me—you may think me jesting,—anything, but serious—but look you, as I live, and as the sun shines,—by Heaven, or by Hell, there is but one escape for you from death, and that is by marriage with my niece. Nothing else can save you; and, but for what I suppose to be her situation, her feelings, and those of Bush Halsey, who has very much the feelings of a girl—but for them, even this choice should not be allowed you. Nay, to show you how large is the concession which I make, I tell you that I now know you to be the son of one of my deadliest enemies, one of those men who have made me what I am, and to whom I owe nothing but undying hate. Your father, in his official capacity, as Judge of the Supreme Court of Alabama, robbed me, by an unrighteous decision, of lands and fortune. Enough, Master Henry Meadows, otherwise Colman, you see where you are, what is known of you, and expected, and what you have to expect. You see the men are in waiting, the cord is ready, and you are already under the tree from which you may be suspended. It has borne as stout a man before."

He turned from me as he spoke, and joined the two men who were conversing at a little distance, said a few words to them, pointed towards me, then disappeared in the wood. But a few moments had elapsed, when he again came in sight, and approached me.

"Your answer, Henry Meadows?"

The smile had disappeared from his features. The face was savage and stern in the extreme. There was nothing there of encouragement, and during his absence my own reflections were of a confused and conflicting character. I need not say that I could not convince myself of the earnestness of the man—I could not persuade myself, that such a destiny was really contemplated for me. My pride determined my course. Was I to be made a laughing-stock, a butt—pointed at as one scared into marriage—led to the altar, through dread of the halter!—even the jingle of the words suggested itself to me at the moment, and the thought that such a jingle would commend the anecdote, in future days at my expense, contributed to strengthen me in my resolution of defiance. My answer was ready.

"I defy you, Sir. Do with me as you please, but you shall not force me to your purpose."

He hesitated—gazed at me for a moment, as I fancied, with an expression of chagrin, and then replied:—

"Very well, young man,—as *you* please! I have done all that I could—more than I ever expected to do to save any one caught in your situation. Your blood be upon your own head. Ho! fellows!"

He waved his hand and the subordinates drew nigh.

"Are you ready? Secure your man!"

In the twinkling of an eye, I was caught up and placed upon my feet, while the fellow named Warner, adjusted the defiling cord about my neck, and, with the end in his hand, proceeded to climb the tree under which I stood. I writhed in my bonds—I could not struggle, for hand and feet were equally secured. But my writhing was in vain. Indeed, so well fastened had I been, that, but for the support of one of the outlaws, I could not have kept my feet. The moment was one of unmixed horror. I began to fear that the farce was to become a tragedy. I looked searchingly into the face of the outlaw, but it expressed nothing but the most dogged determination. The sun, at the same instant, threw a golden crown upon the brow of a towering pine, some thirty yards in advance of the spot where I stood. I shivered! Where *was* Bush Halsey? Where Helen? My head seemed to swim. I was growing blind. Father, mother!—could this all be true! was I thus doomed! Torn from you, to see you never more! I felt that my senses were insecure—that I could no longer depend upon them,—but I could hear—hear every syllable, every breathing. That one faculty seemed to grow doubly acute at the expense of all the rest. There was a whispering among the accessories. Then came the deep but low words of the principal.

"Run him up! There's no use to wait. He's pluck to the last. He'll die game!"

I felt the motion—my feet were gone from under me. I strove to cry aloud, but the words subsided into a husky murmur, and I resigned myself—how—with what grace—with what hope—with what thoughts, if any,—to the last terrible change!—when, sudden, I heard a cry—a piercing shriek—I knew the tones of that voice—I knew the nature of that cry! The voice was Helen's,—the cry—oh! God! it was the lost woman's appeal—for mercy, mercy, mercy! I too strove to echo the cry, but I was choking. I could hear the hollow gurgling of the breath in my own throat—I could feel it!—That was all!

CHAPTER THIRTEEN

I was conscious of a sudden but not unpleasant concussion. I awakened, opened my eyes, and found myself upon the ground, with Helen clinging to me, and plucking at the cord about my neck,—while the outlaw was contending almost violently with her father. I understood the affair in a few moments. Bush Halsey still held in his grasp the knife with which he had smote the cord by which I was suspended. I had been rescued at the last moment—rescued, it was very evident from what I then saw, without any participation in the act by the outlaw. He still appeared resolute upon my death, and, by the numerous gathering of ruffians by whom he was surrounded, and who seemed only to await his final orders, I felt very certain that the dreadful scene must be renewed. I spare the arguments and expostulations of Bush Halsey. I say nothing of the tears and entreaties of Helen.

"Let him submit—let him obey!—let him act as a man of honor!"— was the final answer of the outlaw.

"He will—he will submit!" was the cry of Helen—poor girl—not knowing what was the requisition.

"Give him time—*treat* him as a man of honor!" was the answer of her father.

The tears of Helen—her beauty—the passionate and unmeasured interest which she expressed in my fate—no longer restrained by the dread of her uncle,—the awe of her father, or the natural apprehension and modesty of her sex—did more to reconcile me to compliance than did all the violence of the outlaw!

"Hear me," I exclaimed, interrupting the dispute; "—hear me, sir,"— addressing Bud Halsey,—"had you been more reasonable, and less violent at first, all would have been easy. I am willing to marry Helen—nay, should have sought her, in due time, at the hands of her father. It was in pursuit of her that I sought out your retreat in the swamp, and it was in order to obtain more ready admission that I framed the story of a crime which I had never committed. My hands are innocent of blood, and I am no spy upon you. Under the ardent passion which brought me here, I should have regarded the hand of Helen as the dearest blessing which could be bestowed upon me, and I am only sorry that your violence, by wounding my pride, should have prompted me, even for a moment, to reject such a boon. I do not ask for life—I make no such prayer to you—I can die, I trust, like a man—but I am willing to comply with your conditions!"

"Loose him!" was all that Bud Halsey vouchsafed to say, as he turned off.

"Oh! my Henry!" was the exclamation of poor Helen, as she swooned away upon my bosom.

CHAPTER FOURTEEN

But the swoon of joy occasions no apprehensions. My bonds were severed, and Helen recovered, so that we were enabled to return together to the cottage of her father. He was kind to me, but grave. It was not improbable that Bud Halsey had succeeded in filling him with some of the base suspicions which were strong in his own bosom. Helen was happy, with a sort of uneasy happiness. Whether she seemed to doubt the reality of the event, or that she felt that my consent to the marriage with her had been somewhat extorted, in spite of my avowals, I cannot say,—but, though smiling and declaring herself blest, there was a restless, feverish excitability in her action and movements which did not usually mark them. For my own part, I was sore equally in mind and body. The latter had not passed through the humiliating scenes just described without undergoing some hurts and bruises. But these were as nothing to the mental annoyances which the same events had produced. I had been trampled upon—dishonored—my person degraded by the hands of ruffians, and by the shameful and defiling rope. I felt mean and humbled, and, it may be, that, showing something of this feeling, in my intercourse with Helen, I had caused in her that appearance of inquietude which marred, in some degree, the more grateful appearance of her happiness. But I must not linger on this matter. Bud Halsey was a man to move with all imaginable promptness, and that very night he made his appearance at the cottage, accompanied by a young man, decently clad in black, with something of the outward appearance of a Divine. Such he was, if we may be permitted to make certain allowances, of which more hereafter. He was introduced to me as the Rev. Mr. Mowbray —a gentleman of the Episcopal persuasion. He was a fine looking young man of florid complexion, a bright blue eye with a restless roving twinkle,

which betrayed an unsettled and capricious disposition. His temperament
and the general expression of his features, showed the presence of strong,
unregulated passions. Surprised at seeing him where he was, and procured
with so much readiness, I was still more surprised to learn that he was a
regular resident of the swamp—one of the community—sharing in its
spoils, and, possibly, though of this I could say nothing, partaking in all
its miserable practices. The singular moral anomaly of the criminal, influenced by superstition, and insisting upon having a sort of religion of his
own, even while engaged in the grossest violation of all moral and divine
laws, is too well known and of too frequent occurrence, to render necessary here any elaborate metaphysics. Perhaps, the wonder is, that such
contradiction should be found among a Protestant people. In such coun-
tries as Italy and Spain, the anomaly, if still difficult of explanation, is yet,
because of our familiarity with its occurrence, of less startling effect and
character. There, it has been usual to refer it to the mixed influences of a
bad political government, and the habitual training of a priesthood, forever
indefatigable in the maintenance of its powers. The crime is partly the
result of necessity and circumstances, superstition of mixed ignorance and
training. The same anomaly in America, and with the descendants of the
ancient Puritans, must find some other explanation. Here, it was, unde-
niably; and I soon found that the Reverend Mr. Mowbray, was not only
useful (?) where he was, but that there were frequent occasions for his
services. The sick had his prayers, and the burial at which he did not offi-
ciate was a subject of no little dissatisfaction among the living friends of
the deceased. On the Sabbath, when the *business* of the community was not
urgent, his preaching was well attended. Subsequently, I was given to
understand, that, it was owing to the expression of some discontent on the
part of one of the assistants, that I was not to be allowed the ghostly help
of this gentleman, on the morning of my execution, that led to the delay in
carrying into effect the sentence of the Outlaw Chief, and so, accordingly,
to my rescue. Complying with the suggestion of the subordinate, Bud
Halsey sent for his chaplain, and thus my danger became noised abroad,
so as to reach the ears of Helen and her father, in season to bring them to
my rescue. You may take for granted, that, from that moment, I readily
recognised the importance of a regular chaplain to a band of robbers. My
bride made her appearance in all her beauty, and with all the usual
becoming blushes. Beautiful she was, and the simplicity of her costume,
amply set off and distinguished the peculiarity of her charms. I forgot, as
I surveyed her, the painful circumstances which had conducted me to this

event. I thought of nothing but the passion with which she now filled me—how lovely she was in my eyes—how precious to my heart. I took her hand with rapture, and, for a moment, had no feeling but one of unalloyed happiness. But, even as the service proceeded, while my lips uttered the sacred responses, a dark cloud passed over my imagination. My eyes ceased to behold the actual, surrounding objects. I was transported to another region. I beheld another and very different sight. The good old, well ordered, well adorned Hall at Leaside, with all its images of solemnity mixed with comfort, rose up before my glance. My father and my mother—the one sternly contemplative—the other sad, but smiling, as if in spite of the numerous apprehensions that struggled about her maternal heart. Ah! could they conjecture where I stood and how engaged—in what ceremony—so awful, so irrevocable, so important to their son,—so interesting to themselves—in which they were not permitted to partake—of which they were not permitted to know! I felt a growing weakness in my eyes,—mastered my resolution, spoke audibly the last responses, and clasped my bride to my bosom. With the kiss which I then pressed upon her lips, came a crowd of confused thoughts and inquires. I was a husband at eighteen. An outlaw's daughter was my bride. Had I left the home of my father for this? What had I become? What was I to become? What was to be the fruit of this affair? What fate was before me? Was I, too, to become an outlaw? Was I forever cut off from society and my father's home? I could not answer these inquiries, and—which was worse—I could not dismiss them. Was I happy? That was another question, the answer to which must be confided to the future!

CHAPTER FIFTEEN

But youth—the youth which has been accustomed to indulgence—lives so much in the gratification of its passions and desires, that reflection, which is the result of training and habit, does not often disturb the enjoyment of the present moment. As for happiness, this is, at no period, a proper question. We have very little, in this life, to do with happiness. We have only to live as long as we can, endure as sturdily as we can, and do our duty with our best strength and manhood. A lad of eighteen, brought up as I had been, to be very much his own master, is chiefly considerate of the day, and of what it shall bring forth. With a very different signification and commentary, the scripture apothegm is his—sufficient for the day is the evil thereof—and the good also. In boy-language, I was happy, in spite of the momentary misgivings that disturbed me at the altar. I was a husband. I had taken the highest duties of manhood upon me, and this fact was an appeal to my vanity, which thus, in turn, became a minister to my other impulses. My wife was beautiful and accomplished, intelligent and gentle —tender, and full of love for me—giving me hourly proofs, not only that she regarded her happiness as complete, but that she was womanly solicitous of mine. Had all the circumstances of my marriage suited—had it taken place with the family sanction, and had her connections been such as I could have wished them, I could have found no better wife. She, by herself, was all that I could have desired; and, hurt as I had been, in my pride, stung, mortified and harrassed, by the events which preceded my nuptials, my honey-moon was yet without a cloud. Bud Halsey kept out of sight, and, in our little islet and cottage, we revelled in all the intoxicating delight of a first passion gratified. We lay in the sun like two children, thoughtless of the coming on of night, thoughtless of all things but the dear shady solitude which love had peopled with its own ministering forms, all wooing and beautiful, all sweet and musical, all sympathetic and devoted to the tender mood which prevailed equally over the souls of both. Thus we walked and rode—rambled through silent groves, and, sitting on the trunks of fallen trees, under the shade of their mightier descendants, wove into blossoms, the pretty, petty fancies of youth, that might well—at that period—have furnished a similitude for the first garden experience of our luckless ancestors. That honey-moon was certainly an Eden, while it lasted, to us both. But it was not to last. Helen, however, was not the one in our case to pluck the forbidden fruit. The error was mine. I have already said, or shown, that I was of an impetuous, impatient character, not disposed to forego my object, yet soon gratified, and restless after novelty. With such a person, the thing once attained is apt to lose its attractions, and it is sufficient to brush away the gold and beauty from the more delicate forms of human enjoyment, that we grasp them rudely to our embrace. The first enthusiastic burst of passion over, reflection followed, and then recurred to me, in all their force, those vexing and unanswerable questions which had disturbed me at the altar. What had I become? An outlaw? No! But next kin to one! Certainly, should the government of the United States, or of Mississippi, ever find it necessary to send a sufficient force into our swamp retreat, for the purpose of rooting out its profligate possessors, I must share their obloquy and punishment;—and, even if this fate were not to be apprehended, was the doom less humiliating and painful to which I was now apparently fated. It was forbidden me to leave the swamp! I had not even the rogue's privilege, but, as I refused to participate in the deeds of the outlaws, I was regarded as one not only not to be trusted, but one to be watched. The melancholy prospect was before me of wasting my days in a region in which I was a prisoner—denied even the indulgences of the reprobates around me, and with no hope of a change for the better, unless by qualifying myself for the privileges of the ruffian, in the commission of his crimes. There was no outlet to society or ambition. I could neither hope for the external resources, nor for the distinctions of the world. My talents were denied a field of action. I was to rust disused, a sword in the scabbard, a shield against the wall,—the blood-steed chafing in the stable, the mountain bird beating his wings against the bars of his cage. These reflections naturally followed, when the delights of my new condition had become familiar. Even love is a food that can satisfy few men. It is the blanc-mange, the syllabubs, the comfits, in the great feast of life. But we must beware how we would make a meal of it. It is to be taken sparingly after other meats, and by way of giving them a relish. The only food which never cloys the human spirit, is the prosecution of our daily tasks, in obedience to the natural tendencies of our intellect, and our training. These tasks performed, love consoles us in the shade, binds up our wounds, soothes us in our prostration and defeat, and cheers us with song and sentiment. But as we neither want song nor consolation always, so we may suffer love to wait for us in the shade, while we follow our employments in the sun. By attending to this wholesome rule, we shall discover, that, while the burden of labor diminishes, love undergoes increase; and, from a sickly and somewhat affected damsel, becomes a bright-eyed, cheerful matron, who rears our children with fruitful breakfast, and sees that dinner is ready for us, at the proper hour, when we return from work. But I did not philosophize after this fashion, until long afterwards. In that heyday of my hot youth, and while that first—would it were the last!—struggle was going on, I simply felt and deplored the ennui, without undertaking to ascertain what were its true sources. Had my reflective powers been equal to this, I should probably have been the better for it. But, as it was, seemingly remediless as the condition of things appeared, I was miserable, without the hope of redress. The ardency of my love lessened, and, instead of now going forth with Helen, I stole forth more frequently alone. I wandered off into the deepest woods, and wearied at every step, with myself and everything around me, I still felt how much more wearisome it was to return. Still, I strove to hide from my wife, the discontent of which I was now myself fully conscious. I was generous enough, and man enough, to endeavor to conceal from her the signs of that inquietude, which I too well knew she would ascribe to my lessening attachment. In her presence I strove to be cheerful, to smile, to meet her eye with the same expression of love in mine, which it had been so easy a task with me to exhibit until now. Nor was it always difficult to simulate this appearance. She was so really beautiful, with eyes of such dewy brightness, so gentle, so yielding and dependant, that, really, I could not but curse the capricious nature which had grown dissatisfied, so soon, with a creature so truly excellent and charming. Still, she hung upon my arm, yielded herself upon my bosom, sung to me in deep embowering woods, and by the petty chafing streams that ran through our swamp fastnesses, and still I thought at moments, that I ought to be, and was, satisfied and happy.

But these gleams were only transient. Love, *alone,* has no means of continuing its excitements, after conquest. With this event life begins, with all its solemn duties. Unless these duties provoke the fitting performances —unless the man then brings into exercise all the energies of his intellectual nature, and addresses them to the business which seems to be most particularly called for by the tendency of his *morale*—he cannot well be said to live, and none of his enjoyments will be lasting. This must be the fate of all persons brought up in idleness. Life, with such, must be a sort of mill-service, a perpetual rounding of the circle in a beaten track, which, as it demands no mental exercise, furnishes no mental supply, keeps up no mental life, and leaves the intellectual nature as thoroughly blind as horses are said to become, habituated to the same motive service which as afforded us the comparison above. But a truce to these reflections, which I did not then make. My wife began to discern the change in me. What change is there, however slight, in the man she loves, which the woman will not discern? I soon saw that she *felt* the change. Perhaps, it was no small proof of my own continued attachment, that I could so soon discern that she had made the discovery. Of course I did my best to lessen this impression. I renewed my efforts to appear happy—we resumed our walks together—followed the same streams, sat beneath the same shade,—but we both felt that it was now a task to pursue the same life, which was once a pleasure only. The green and the freshness seemed to me to have gone from life—the glory and the gladness—we felt the misery which the departure had occasioned, but knew not, in our ignorance of heart and life, where to look for the remedy. It was soon very evident to me, that her father beheld the change. He looked more gravely when we met,—more sadly—but without severity. On the contrary, his endeavors to console and to conciliate me were redoubled; and when in his society, I generally found myself more cheerful, and if not more reconciled to my imprisonment, at least more easily inclined, for the moment, to dismiss it from my thoughts. That he ascribed my demeanor to any change in my regards for his daughter, I did not imagine. He knew me better than I did myself. My own conscience reproached me with such a change. He, more wisely, ascribed it all to the natural impatience of my mind, under the novel restraints to which it was subjected—restraints, which not only deprived me all opportunity for its exercise, but denied me to see those friends and connections, in whom I was naturally so deeply interested. As for poor Helen, she was still so loving, so considerate, so desirous to win me to pleasure, to see me happy—and failing,—so sad,—that, when not thinking absolutely and only of myself, my heart smote me for its coldness to her. Coldness shall I call it? No! it was not coldness. I had not then any idea that any woman could be half so dear to me as she was, even in those moments when I felt least satisfied. But she was not to know this.

My discontent increased, and at length settled down into positive clouds and gloom. I no longer made any effort to conceal it, and it was some consolation to me that my wife, with a prudence which is seldom exercised by wives, never once called upon me to account for it. She was content to do her best to cheer me, to prove that her love for me had not lessened, and she left to the delicate unpremeditated attentions of a fond heart, and tender solicitude, to heal those hurts, which any attempt to probe might only have rendered worse.

CHAPTER SIXTEEN

Meanwhile, I had become somewhat intimate with Mr. Mowbray, the reverend gentleman by whom I had been married. I had met him in some of my rambles, and as he was a person of invincible self-esteem, he had contrived to keep with me, in spite of the evident coolness which I manifested towards him. His adroitness finally broke down my barriers of reserve, and I listened to him, after awhile, with tolerable patience,—the unfavorable impressions of my mind gradually giving way, the more I was brought in contact with the offensive object. This is one of the most fruitful dangers which beset young men. I had reason afterwards to believe that Bud Halsey had instructed Mowbray to throw himself in my way, with the view to bringing me round to his purposes. This young man spoke with a vivacity which was very much akin to wit. He was sprightly, forcible and pungent in his remarks, frequently novel and always audacious. That he was thoroughly unprincipled, need not be said, when it is remembered what life he led and what principles he professed to teach. Perhaps, there is no hypocrisy so complete and lamentable, as that of the professor of religion, having the care of others, yet daily, and daringly, indulging in the most unscrupulous practices of sin.

"You are cool to me," he said one day when I was more than usually depressed by the circumstances of my situation. He had joined me when I least looked for, and least wished, any such companionship.

"Why should we not be friends?" he continued, without giving me time to answer. "Here we are, both of us young fellows, neither wanting in stuff for conversation, why should we not be more frequently together? As we have a little world of our own here, why should we not make the most of it?"

"You may—you should," was my answer. "But you forget, it is your world, not mine."

"Make it yours—why not?"

"Thank you, but I have no taste for cutting throats or purses."

"Pshaw! I do not mean that. There are enough to do that without requiring either you or me. My taste as little inclines to it as yours."

"Why then are you here?"

"A truant disposition—like your own, perhaps. But now that we are both here, whether from choice or necessity, I am for making the most of the situation. Why should not you? Why, for example, should you mope alone in these woods, when you might have company?"

"Have I not?" Are you not with me?"

"Yes; but I verily believe that you would rather my room than my company."

"You could scarcely believe this, yet continue to give it me."

"You forget my profession!" he answered, with a laugh. "My religion compels me to seek the unhappy—my humility prevents me from heeding their rebuffs. I am for saving you, my friend, in your own spite,—for consoling you when, perhaps, you would prefer to drain the cup of bitterness to the dregs, through sheer obstinacy,—and for giving you my good company, always, when you are most oppressed with your own."

"Do you not incur some risk in this liberality? Intrusion does not always get off with a simple rebuff."

"Ah! You must not suppose I carry my religion to excess. I do not tell you that I turn the other cheek that it may be smitten also. I have not yet reached that point of patience and forbearance, when it is ageeable to set up for a martyr. I have still a taste of the old leaven in me, and can lay on as well as my neighbor. But there need be no quarrel between us. Time sometimes hangs heavily on my hands here, as it evidently does on yours. If we were to meet oftener, it might weigh more lightly upon both. I have usually been considered a good fellow as a companion, and you seem a lad of mettle. You have sense and spirit. Let us see if we cannot help each other through the swamp—no bad figure for representing the dull days in this quarter. Come, now, let me be your guide for the next half hour, and I will show you some retreats here which, I suspect, you have never seen before. What say you?"

I suffered him to lead me on. Indeed, I was now not only indifferent to the route which I should take, but somewhat regardless of the character of my companion. The last few weeks had made me tolerably reckless, and setting aside some of my scruples as I proceeded with him, I abruptly asked him for his history. I was anxious to get some insight into a character which seemed so curiously compounded.

"My history!" he answered. "You shall have it. It will scarcely interest you, but will do you good. You smile?"

"Yes!—why should you care whether it will do me good or not?"

"You mistake me somewhat. I have no wish to do you harm."

"What! Not to involve me in your meshes—make me an outlaw like yourself?"

"Pshaw, no! I care for this neither one way nor the other. My fault, indeed, is want of sympathy with my race."

"Why do you wish society, then,—companionship—why seek mine?"

"Simply because I am selfish. Selfishness makes good companionship. I seek you for myself—for my own enjoyment, not yours;—though I shall have no sort of objection that you should gain by the communion. But, you will know me better when you have heard my story. Here, we are secure. We have quite a pleasant shade. The trees arch here in cathedral fashion. The sun scarcely penetrates, except in little droplets of light, and the effect is very much such as we should suppose it would produce through the stained windows of a gothic abbey. The breeze comes up very pleasantly from that water. Your wanderings have brought you here before."

The spot was very beautiful, with an interest derived entirely from the foliage, and the mixed effect of shadow and subdued sunlight. There was no inequality in the landscape. The ground was perfectly level, with a slight slope to the water's edge. The creek wound semi-circularly about us, and along the opposite edges was lined with a thick fringe of canes, from whence shot up the gigantic spire of cotton-wood tree or pine. We sat down upon the shaft of a fallen tree, and, after a few preliminaries, my companion began his story as follows:

Mr. Mowbray's Story

You see in me an instance of the injurious effects of endeavoring to force goodness into the heart by a sort of hot-house process. Unless by miracle, by the direct intervention of Deity himself, you cannot make a man a saint before his time. There must be some long preliminary courses. There must be trials and preparations, by which to subdue stubborn tendencies, irregular passions, and a dogged, inflexible will. I do not pretend to set before you the sort of training which should be employed for this purpose. It is enough that I had none of it; and, with just enough of prudence—cunning, perhaps, would be the proper word—I suffered myself to be converted into an apostle, before I had ever thought to overcome the natural desire which every man is supposed to have to be a sinner. I was born of good family, in one of the oldest of our northern cities. I need scarcely tell you that the name I bear, is not the one to which I was born. I was tenderly nurtured and well-educated. My father was not only distinguished in the social, but in the intellectual world. He was a man of profound scientific and literary acquirements,—highly and equally esteemed for his moral virtues and mental superiority. It was, perhaps, my misfortune in particular that he died, just at that period when, emerging from boyhood into youth, my training required the firm hand and the calm thought of experienced wisdom. My boyhood gave signs of intellectual promise. My youth had other developments. I was wild and vicious, full of blood and passions—eager in the attainment of my object, and not over-scrupulous—speaking within certain limits—of the process by which this was to be done. But the tenderness of relatives, and the sympathies of friends, kindly charged all these developments to the exuberance of youth. I was simply sowing those wild-oats, which, I am disposed to think, must be sown by all men, sooner or later, at some period in their lives. The misfortune is, that, in my case, sufficient time was not allowed me to sow my tares, when I was required to enter upon another sort of harvest. It is scarcely to be wondered at if the tares and wheat came up pretty equally together.

Our family was reduced in fortune and straitened after my father's death, to such a degree, that it became necessary—painful necessity!—that hereafter the sons should sow that they might reap. We were all required to work for our bread, and the question was, in what way we should encounter a necessity so humiliating, without losing the rank and consideration of gentlemen. This inquiry, of course, involved a farther necessity, not only of finding a proper employment, but one neither mechanical nor laborious—one that would neither soil the hands nor lessen the leisure. Two of my brothers were already lawyers, one was a physician, and as both these professions were crowded, it was unanimously concluded among my friends and relatives, that I was to be a parson. Not that I had shewn any of those moral qualities, which would naturally incline a devout parent to see a future saint in the son. I was neither humble in spirit, forbearing in my anger, nor gentle in my deportment. I had nothing devotional about me. I had the most indomitable will,—I had the most fierce, selfish, and passionate desires. I had no single requisite for the business of the pulpit, but such as belonged to the simple intellect. As I do not scruple to declare my moral deficiencies, so I do not hesitate to avow my intellectual adequacy to the work before me. I was warm, animated, fluent,—intense, in my earnestness, to the last degree, and, in the employment of illustration and figure, equally forcible and ready. I was destined, so every body said,—regarding nothing but my mental endowments—to figure as a new Boanerges in the church.

But, at first, I was just as unwilling as I was unprepared, to enter upon a duty for which my mind had no sympathy. If I inclined to anything in particular, it was to the law. To the forum I looked as to the scene of my future triumphs—as to the field of my future eminence and fame. But I was made to see with the eyes of others. I was shewn the crowded state of the bar. I was shewn the struggling and always half distressed situation of my brothers, neither of whom had, as yet, earned the salt for his porridge. They were still an incumbrance on the very little property which the misfortunes of the family had spared to my mother. Nobody seemed to regard the moral requisites of the Churchman, as at all necessary. Nothing, at least, was said on this part of the subject. It was chosen for me as a handicraft —a trade—by which I was to jump into a snug living, and have the farther privilege of choosing, as my own peculiar property, one of the richest ewes of my flock. These results were continually spoken of, as a matter of course, by all around me. They formed a familiar topic with the community. Religion had become so much of a profession, among laity and clergy, that the trading results were habitually looked to, by both parties, as a legitimate subject of consideration. In old communities, which have been, from immemorial time, distinguished for high social tone, the maintenance of social appearances becomes, finally, the leading object with all parties; and all that is then requisite with the individual is, that he should respect his own cloth. It does not matter that he should not deserve to wear it. The only important particular is, that he should wear it with decency. The rule holds with religion as with medicine or law—it is ranked with these as an ordinary means of employment, and by many, as one of the most inferior. Indeed, one of my objections to adopting this profession, arose from hearing it so frequently spoken of as one that required little or no ability. The common saying among us, was, 'when a fellow is too stupid to be lawyer or doctor, you must make him a parson.' There was room for the sarcasm. We had many boobies in the pulpit. There was little eloquence and less thought. Some of our divines were able men, but they had grown tired of warring against those feminine tastes in the audience, which called for little more than common-places and declamation. Women, of whom most of our American audiences are composed, do no little towards the degradation of the clergy. It requires but little skill and management among them, to win the reputation of great piety; and still less ability, to secure that of eloquence and talent. I have frequently amused myself, during my brief career in the pulpit, in preaching nonsense-sermons, that were simply complicate and high-sounding, larded at frequent intervals, with biblical phrases, with which they were commonly acquainted. I have observed that, on such occasions, my preaching always gave the most satisfaction. I have always been applauded for these sermons, and more than once called upon to print them,—but I too well knew that what would be tolerated in the pulpit, would never pass the gauntlet of the press,—though, towards the close of my career,—when I was willing to break with my congregation, I was more than half tempted to comply with their wishes, and put forth a volume to show how easily and admirably they had been gulled. But I anticipate.

It was with considerable reluctance that I was brought to regard the wishes of my friends and family with favor. It was only when it became evident that this was the only way in which I could get my bread, and get it buttered too, that I consented. Promises, assurances the most positive, were held out to me, not only of a church, but of a wife, both of them the most elegant and eligible in every point of view. Then there was the influence, the authority, which the cloth exercised;—and,—this was my own thought, and that which rendered the suggestions of my friends more palatable—then there was the distinction, the eminence to be attained by the pressing, persevering and highly endowed intellect. Won by all these considerations, I became a student in divinity, put on the grave suit and demeanor, and went to my studies with the resolution not to forego the cakes and ale, if they were to be had at the expense only of a little hypocrisy. My character was one of great energy, and might have been of great power, had it been less capricious. As it was, I devoted myself to study with that earnestness which distinguished me in the prosecution of all my plans. I was late and early at my studies. Ambitious, to a very high degree, the goal immediately before me was one of human distinction. My industry and zeal became the popular theme in our little world. Old men looked upon with me wonder—old women with admiration. I was sought by the grave and the seniors of both sexes. I listened with reverence, and when I spoke, dealt in sententious apothegms. I practiced my part with a degree of skill, which, perhaps, was only remarkable for the consistency which my character displayed, in spite of my passions and caprices, during the tedious period of my noviciate. I was successful, and the time arrived when I should take orders and be admitted to the priesthood. The ceremony you have witnessed. I need not describe it. It is enough for me to say, that, solemn as it is, terrible as is the trust which the neophyte undertakes, and awful as appear the responsibilities accruing from his obligations, my mind strove in vain to concentrate its thoughts upon the proceedings. My mind had nothing to do with them. It was communing apart with its own vanities—yearning with its merely human passions, and canvassing, at every interval, the hopes, and fears, and fancies which occupy the spirit of the worldling. But a little distance from me stood a maiden whom my eyes had long singled out as the object of their desires. I saw her not then, but I *felt* that she was there. Pure and meek, she had long before won the affections of one who was neither pure nor meek. Unknown to herself, I had already made a conquest of her. That I *knew*. I was no small judge of the female heart. I had fathomed the intricacies of hers, and resolving that she should be my prize, I had adapted my deportment to those tastes which, I felt assured, distinguished her nature; and, even at that moment when devoting myself, mind and spirit, irrevocably to God and the Redeemer, I thought of neither, except vaguely, uncertainly, and without being at all touched by the profound depth of the obligation which my lips had sworn. I thought only of the mortal beauty whose spirit seemed effused about me,—whose presence I felt was near,—whose eyes, I well knew, watched every step in the progress of the ceremony, with the intense interest of the purest human love. I was ordained—I had attained one of the objects of my hypocritical endeavor, and the struggle now was for the rest. Did I attain them? Did I doubt of their attainment? You shall hear!

Yet, do not misunderstand me. If you suppose that I did not strive after religion, when I had once undertaken the study, you will do me injustice. It may be that I did not strive enough,—with all my heart, with all my mind, and with all my strength, as we are required—but I certainly did not set out to persevere in a merely cold system of hypocrisy. I was not unwilling to become what I wished to profess. I strove, I studied, I thought, I asked. It is not improbable that in study, thought and inquiry, I sometimes forgot prayer. I did not pray enough. I never acquired the first most necessary frame of mind. I had no humility, and this want,—had not my congregation been wilfully, and beyond redemption, blind,—must have betrayed me long before I wilfully betrayed myself. I was myself deceived. I sometimes fancied my condition of mind was good—was what it should be. This was during my noviciate. I was never deceived in this manner after my assumption of the duties of the priesthood. No! no! I knew myself by this time, and the struggle thence was simply to keep the real nature from any and every exhibition inconsistent with that which I had put on. But of this hereafter.

My friends kept their promises. They procured me a church, and a noble congregation. I was at once installed into a good living, and, very soon after, chose, from among my flock, the fair and truly good creature, upon whom, so long a season, my eyes had been set. She did not, with feminine subtlety, endeavor to hide from me the joy she felt when I declared my passion for her. 'She was too, too happy.' Such were the words muttered in my bosom, as she yielded herself to my embrace. We were married, and with herself she brought me a handsome property. Was I satisfied? Was I happy? No! I had reaped the reward of my toils,—I had gained all the objects which had been proposed to me, when I first commenced my career of hypocrisy. Station, fortune, fame!—for I had grown famous in our little world—but, I did not deceive myself! I was not only not happy, but I was ill at ease. The constraint upon my nature was a bondage which I yearned to throw off. I was like the captive in the toils! True, I was surrounded by plenty—beauty was in my arms—fortune at my feet—crowds of admirers followed in my steps—troops of friends gathered at my bidding—my voice could still or rouse the multitude— my name was honored wherever spoken—but *I lived a lie!*—and every moment of breath and being was a pang. I do not say that my moral sense revolted at this condition. No! it was my blood, my passions, which, restrained, in order to the acquisition of an object, threatened momently to revenge themselves for the unnatural and uncongenial bondage into which my will had forced them.

Meanwhile, had the theatre of my mind been such as it could have chosen, I should have been content. My mind was fully exercised. In the habit of intensifying on every subject, I was necessarily a most enthusiastic preacher. Never was the vehemence of true zeal and genuine piety more life-like than mine. They attributed this vehemence to my zeal and piety, when it was only the natural working of my blood. In a disputation in behalf of atheism, I should have been equally vehement. It was the characteristic of my temperament. But nobody inquired into this. It was enough that I kept them from sleeping;—that, all animation myself, I enlivened them. Of course, nobody who goes to church applies to himself the denunciations of the preacher. The simple fact of church-going seems sufficiently to satisfy the ordinary mind; and people fancy they are in a very comfortable sort of trim for heaven when they yield audible responses to the preacher, and never forget to make their genuflexions at the appropriate moment. I saw and understood all this, and was by no means unsparing of the scourge. I laid it on with heavy hand, and, assured in my own heart of my own miserable hypocrisy, this conviction furnished an additional reason why I should cry aloud, and spare not, in dealing with the sinfulness of others. In this sort of excitement I lived—I drew my breath. My blood demanded excitements, and, dammed up in its natural tendencies, was forced to find outlet and utterance through other avenues. Was there a controversy with another sect or church, I headed it;—was there a new mission to be established, I counselled it, urged it, and compelled it. Furious in my struggles, I made a battle field wherever I came, and while all were delighted and wondering at my zeal in the cause of the Redeemer, I brought nothing but religious uproar, and confusion, and disputation where I appeared.

Had my congregation been only half-witted,—had they but bestowed upon the subject but half the thought which the meanest of them gave to his ordinary worldly concerns—they must have more than suspected my sincerity. The very excess of my fervor, must have made them doubt its purity and source. But a few years before—not five,—I had been notoriously a very vicious youth—noted for excesses, and recognizing, with difficulty, any restraint. On a sudden, the change had been effected. Now, it is not denied that this change of heart, can be effected by the ruling powers of Providence, at any moment,—in a moment,—in the twinkling of an eye,—but this change of heart, must subdue the heart,—must teach patience, humility, and moderation. The individual must remember, with horror, his own past offences, and must, in fear and trembling, approach those of others. If such a change produces any external results at all, it must be in this very particular. It must lead to great toleration. Mercy, not denunciation, will be the language of the newly reformed—humility, not arrogance,—patience, not imperiousness. There was no such show in me. On the contrary, never did self-appointed legate, more freely use God's thunder. The Pope was not more imperious, when, setting his feet upon the necks of princes, he insisted that the act was done in his two-fold character, of man and father,—than was I in dealing with those very faults and vices in others, in which, but a little while before, I had notoriously indulged myself. But I had no help. My passionate and imperious nature was resolute to speak out, and this was the only way in which it could exercise itself, consistently with the part which I was now compelled to play, to the mockery of God and man alike.

But there was a change at hand. In the midst of my successes—when I stood in the regards of the community as little less than a God—when thousands followed, and, without knowing or suspecting it, hundreds of poor women worshipped me—when my eloquence was most brilliant, my exhortations most urgent, my severities and rebukes most pungent, and excoriating—my secret was discovered. It could not be concealed from one who had been among the first to follow—to worship me and to love—

my wife! Without being a philosopher, her moral and religious instincts were true;—there are religious instincts in every nature, to be brought out by education;—to her my secret was betrayed on numerous occasions. Seeing me at home—in disabille—without those restraints of decorum in which I garbed myself for the encounter with others, she soon had sufficient proof that I was no saint. My passions, my temper,—my real nature—was not to be hid from her, and when the applauses of others filled her ears—when her friends eulogized my virtues, and congratulated her on her good fortune, in the possession of such a saint,—she only wept. She was no more to be flattered into happiness, than she was to be deceived by externals. She could not conceal her convictions and feelings from me. Long did she strive to do so, but her Christian spirit triumphed. She revealed to me the extent of her discoveries, her fear, her wretchedness,— she implored me to repent in sincerity, or, at least, to forbear the profession which could only be dishonored by my hypocrisy. She did not use this language, but this was the substance of what she said. She employed the gentlest forms of speech, such as were dictated by a still devoted heart and an ardent passion. But I flung her from me. She had doubly offended me, as she had discovered my secret, and, in doing so, had shewn me that the love which she bore for me, did not amount to the adoration which alone I sought. My desires were of that imperious sort, that would admit of nothing qualifying in the homage which I received. The whole heart for me, or none,—and it must be a thoroughly confiding heart, a perfect faith, never questioning, always submitting, always assured—with the old-time loyalty of the serf—that the king could do no wrong. I flung her from me,—it was the Sabbath,—and, proceeding to my pulpit, I made the high ceilings echo again with the intensity of my exhortations. I was never more eloquent. I was stung, provoked, exasperated,—and, at such moments, my vehemence was a torrent that defied all let or hindrance. But my wife went not with me. From that day forth she was never more an auditor of mine. She prayed at home—in secret, and, I well knew, that her prayers were for me. But her firmness vexed me. Her superiority wounded me. Her keenness of remark annoyed me. She was no longer to be deceived; and, whatever might be her external bearing—and it was exemplary,—and I felt that, though perhaps, secure of her obedience,—I was no longer secure of her respect.

Thus passed several months, and, with my domestic relations such as I have described them,—the constraints of my public career became more irksome. The redeeming circumstances by which I had been consoled, the applause and admiration—though not by any means lessened—began to stale upon my estimation. The field was a confined one—the audience was the same—I had already heard their wonder—it no longer gave me pleasure. It no longer rewarded my eloquence or stimulated my exertions. I felt, more and more, with the progress of every day, the intensest cravings for my freedom. *That* denied, what was all in possession? The passion grew to morbidness, and, but for one event, the catastrophe which finally happened, would at once have taken place. My wife brought me a child, a fine, fair son, that, for the time, by appealing to the more ordinary human feeling, reconciled me somewhat to the restraints of my position. Caressing him, I felt how sweet it was to be a father. My wife seized the moment when she saw me most tenderly engaged in fondling him, to renew her entreaties and exhortations,—and so meekly, so tenderly, so like an angel, —that, had my passions been less like that of a demon, I must have been overcome. I answered her gloomily, almost fiercely, and left the room. It is not easy for you to imagine my feelings from this slight survey of my position. No man, whatever be his nature, feels quite at ease in daily communion of the confiding and affectionate character, with those whom he defrauds. Such was the relation in which I stood with my flock. Besides, mine was a diseased nature, and the fraud was one of the most extreme and vital character. Every encounter with my congregation was productive of a struggle, and you may suppose many more struggles of conscience and prudence must have grown out of a position which exposed me to some of the most peculiar temptations. The office which I held is one of peculiar and scarcely limitable privileges and powers. The trial must be a great one, even where the professor is a really good man, conscious only of the best purposes. What was mine? That I yielded—that I did not always struggle,— that I frequently abused my trust, you may conjecture—it is not for me to relate. But, usually, the vicious man, if busy without, in a practice which wrongs his neighbor, is not often met at home with those rebukes and reproaches, on that account, which he does not hear abroad. If he himself does not offend against his wife, she is very apt, readily, to forgive his offences against others. Not so, mine! Her love for me, based originally on her convictions of my piety, was not sufficient to keep her silent when my secret was in her possession. Her love for purity was greater. Her loyalty to God was superior to that which she felt for me; and for this, I was indignant. Half-formed calculations, plans and purposes, of remedy and relief, began to fill my brain; and, at this time, had my sermons been scanned by a suspicious judgment, they would have been found distinguished by a tone of bitterness and sarcasm, if not contempt, which, addressed as they were to my audience, would have tended, in no great degree, to render them satisfied either with their seats or my eloquence. It was then, too, that I amused myself at their expense, with those nonsense sermons, of which I have already given you some idea. You may imagine it did not increase my estimate of the value of their judgments, even when shown in my own eulogies, when I found them particularly delighted with these specimens of rigmarole. Having reached this stage, can you not guess the rest? Having gained all that I could gain by the constraints which I had put upon my nature—having found these gains unsatisfactory, if not worthless—what had I to bind me to my home? My wife pitied rather than loved me, and the flock by which I might have been loved, was the object of my own scorn and dislike. I left them,—and, with a sense of joy in my new found liberty, which I should find myself at a loss for language to describe. You cannot conceive the satisfaction which I felt in writing a farewell letter to the heads of the church. I revenged myself in that for long months of bondage. I filled it with passages of most withering scorn. I avowed my own hypocrisy, but reminded them of theirs, and asserted my better claims to God's favor, by the very proceeding by which, in the estimation of the world, I had renounced God himself—namely, my resignation from a station to which, as I alleged, scarcely one of us had any proper pretensions. That I had ceased to be a hypocrite, was a sufficient reason to hope for my final regeneration as an honest man. This step was taken in connection with several others. I renounced home, and wife, and child, at the same moment. It was some proof, perhaps, that I was not utterly reckless, when I felt unwilling any longer to look them in the face. I had means,—I had money,—and, passing to New Orleans, I found an element of sufficient elasticity for my moral nature, in its various theatres of pleasure and dissipation. I took ample revenge for my long abstinence. I drank—and gamed—and, to make a long story short, I am here! You look at me with horror! Hear me! I believe there is a God, and I believe there is a devil. We are the subjects of one or the other, and if one rejects our services, as not worthy of him, it is scarcely possible to suppose that the other will not have need of them. We cannot well war with the direction given us. Miracles may do much, but there is little wisdom in waiting for them. I would hope if I could— but I despair. I toil with the conviction that I am a doomed man—doomed from my birth. The appalling feeling is over me, that under this doom I will perish—perish forever! That this high spirit is utterly outcast—that this high thought, which I have betrayed, and this glorious mind which I have defrauded of its privileges, and degraded to evil purposes—will become extinct. I shudder with the thought of annihilation, since it is only the hope of immortality that moves the moral, and satisfies the intellectual nature. You see that I do not exult in this depravation. You see that I relate the story of the past without pleasure! That I suffer! That I feel the folly and the sin of all that miserable boy-career, begun in narrow schemes, and finishing in shocking perversion. You ask why I do not change—why I stubbornly live in sin—why I do not regret, repent, retrieve? What if I tell you of my tears, my prayers, my repentance? I do weep! I do repent! But what is repentance that does nothing but weep? This is mine! I do nothing! My repentance is without results! I cannot pray—I cannot toil—in any work of good! There is a terrible power that denies me—that keeps me back from the very first performances of repentance! I dare not ask what is this power! I only feel that its presence is upon me, baffling my purpose, and mocking at all my hopes! It never can be withdrawn! I am not suffered to approach the throne of God—I am doomed, utterly doomed of heaven!

———————————

Thus ended this extraordinary narrative. The speaker had risen, long before he came to the close, under the exciting character of what he said. He now sat down, but, suddenly, again rose to his feet, as if to depart. There had been a very decided and remarkable change in his appearance, during its progress. At the beginning, his features had been marked by a good-humored indifference, a sort of easy, careless, good-natured recklessness, which half reconciled me to a person, against whom my prejudices were naturally strong at first. But, as he proceeded, he became excited in his narrative, and very soon illustrated, by his example, the characteristic of intensity, which he insisted upon as so prominent in his temperament. At the close, and when he pronounced those scarcely coherent, but very solemn sentences, with which he abruptly finished his narrative, his features grew dark. There was a wild and troubled expression in his eyes, which were sombre and restless, as some deep pool which secret fires are troubling. His lips were parted and the corners drooped, while his breast labored with emotions, which must have aptly corresponded with those which his words expressed. The awful thoughts which had fallen from him, if really entertained, were well calculated to awaken the most fearful agonies in his breast. To what a dreadful approach had he come! Upon what a precipice did he stand; and how wretched and demoniac the sort of philosophy from which he proposed to draw his consolation. We may suppose that when Lucifer broke finally with Heaven, and had no more hope, that he consoled himself by some such philosophy. He was not in the mood, nor I in the vein, for farther conversation. At such a moment, any attempt at exhortation on my part, would have been as injudicious as impertinent. We walked together for a space in silence. I need not say how much my respect for this unhappy person had increased, from hearing his story. I say respect,—because it was now evident to me, that his position and practices were not such as were agreeable to him. He was wretched, and the worm of remorse was already busy at his vitals. In this was my hope on his behalf, though it was evidently not his own. There is some hope for the sinner who is miserable,—none for him who is insensible. As we reached the place where he had joined me and we were about to separate, he turned to me,—and said warningly:

"I had forgotten! Be cool, be cautious, in what you design. Do nothing hastily! Bud Halsey already suspects you, and he is master here. His brother can do nothing. Be warned! I would befriend you."

"What do you mean?" I demanded.

"Nothing but what I have said. It is what *you mean,* that is the question. Bud Halsey has noticed your discontent. He suspects its cause. He suspects you, your wife, his brother! He has his eye upon you all. Beware!"

He disappeared in another instant, and, musing upon what he said, I made my way homewards.

CHAPTER SEVENTEEN

What were my designs? The last words,—the warning caution which Mowbray had suggested, produced a closer degree of self-examination than I had ever before undertaken. I had no designs. I was aware of none; but that it was expected of me that I should entertain some, naturally led me to them. Was I to be fettered in this way all my life;—my youth lost;—my better days and energies swallowed up in such a miserable sphere of imbecility as that in which I found myself—release from which seemed only obvious on terms of still worse degradation? The thought was inexpressibly humiliating. From humiliation I got strength—I got resolve. My purpose suddenly adopted, was to fly from my prison—to devote all my energies, all my intellect, to this one purpose. But art was necessary—cunning—I was to foil the devil at his own game—with his own weapons. To this resolve I rushed, ere I reached the cottage of Bush Halsey. There, I found my wife awaiting me. I threw off the air of despondency which had possessed me. The simple determination to be doing something had its effect in relieving me from the mental prostration under which I had suffered. I met Helen with a degree of buoyancy which I had never shewn before. My rude laughter, and violent mirth, made her look at me with surprise, but it was a surprise not unmixed with pleasure. She congratulated me and herself upon the change, and, in the belief that I was as happy as she wished me, and quite content with herself—of which my late sullenness had made her somewhat doubtful,—she surrendered herself up to the feeling of joy which, for the time, had neither doubt nor qualification. In these feelings of satisfaction, Bush Halsey shared. He had beheld my despondency with dissatisfaction, and readily divined the cause. But he could see no remedy. He knew his brother—the tyrannical nature, by which himself governed, he governed all others; and, believing that I had no escape from the Swamp, he could only counsel me to the sort of resignation by which he himself was reconciled to it. But the change which my deportment had undergone, if it deceived both himself and daughter, did not long deceive the latter, or she began to doubt the purity and propriety of its origin. Women are close observers, and arrive, by the keenest instincts, at the truth in all things which much affect the objects whom they love. Whatever might be the success of my practice upon others, its tendency was more than doubtful to her, and, after a few weeks, she was less satisfied with my violent good spirits than she had been at first. These alone, perhaps, would not have disquieted her, but, by this time, I had become rather a frequent associate with the outlaw parson. The flexibility of this man was wonderful. He had left me, on the day when I had heard his narrative, looking more like a maniac than a man. Never could I suppose that the same person would ever smile again. The next day, he met me with a bawdy jest. It was one of the characteristics of his temperament to be easily moved by the passing influence, whether grave or gay—a sort of moral character to receive its dark or bright aspects from the colors with which he came into contact. I found him always thus capricious;—at one moment gloomy, even to ferocity, and sometimes touched with a sort of religious fanaticism that would have done honor to the ruggedest bare-bones of the Long Parliament. The next day, he was the courtier—all gravity and smiles, and as loose in his morals as the most reckless cavalier of the Court of Charles the Second—as courtly as Waller, and as licentious as Rochester,—as sentimental sometimes as the one, and again as filthily witty as the other. He realized the extremes of character more suddenly, in the same person, and frequently on the same day, than any other man I ever met. I confess that I was not unfrequently pleased with his society—his wit—his eloquence—his sentiment. He had all upon occasion, and had he been an adroit man, might, I believe, have led me as he pleased. But he was totally devoid of judgment. Had none of that moral prudence which makes the great politician; and, while he won at one moment, he too frequently offended all my tastes, and disgusted me at another. I sought him, however, and this flattered him. I was rather superior as a companion to those with whom he ordinarily associated, and, in the better capacity which I brought to appreciate his merits, he showed himself very accessible on the score of mine. In the new pleasure which I occasionally found in his society,—in the excitement which it afforded and offered me, and in the prosecution of the plan which I had hit upon for extricating myself from the meshes in which I was bound, I sought him frequently. He was not the person to pry very deeply into the sources of the pleasure which he received, nor to analyse those motives in others, the results of which afforded him the society which he desired. He seemed to take for granted, with that vanity which was a large feature in his character, that I sought him because of his intellect. I encouraged the idea, made frequent appeals to his judgment, and, by getting him to dilate upon various passages and portions of his story, directed his thoughts upon himself rather than to mine. In this way I brought not only him, but others, to the conviction that I was fast losing my superior moral standard, and reconciling myself to such as were paramount in the Swamp. Bud Halsey looked on me with more complacency, and not unfrequently contrived to join the parson and myself in the long rambles which we now so frequently took together. He had occasionally a word for me of more particular favor, and took care to confirm, by sentences of mingled sneer and compliment, those impressions, which, he fancied, had been conveyed by my companion to my mind.

"You will be a man yet!" was his frequent phrase, as he left us for his other objects. "Your eyes are opening."

But the circumstances which gave him satisfaction now, afforded none to his brother, Bush Halsey, or my wife. Their attachment to me, as I have intimated rather than said, arose in part from the tenacious firmness with which I had held to my virtues. I have endeavored to show that Bush Halsey was the victim of his own imbecility, as well as of circumstances. A good man, meaning well, and with an excellent mind, he was yet controlled entirely by the superior will of his brother—a man of inferior intellect—of bad habits and character—but of indomitable energies, and unrelaxing determination. It was his own misery that, unwilling to face bankruptcy and its consequences, in the civilized community in which he had lived like a nobleman, he was yet compelled to rear up his only child—a girl—in contact with the wretched profligates among whom I found him. But, once a slave, such a man always remains a slave. From the moment that he yielded to the suggestions of his brother, and fled from his creditors to the wilderness, from that moment, he yielded himself up to a bondage, from which he did not now hope to set himself free. But that his child should grow up in such a situation, with no escape from such a life, was to him a source of perpetual suffering. Elegant himself in his tastes, he had tutored hers, with a degree of watchfulness and skill which can better be conjectured than detailed and it was with a feeling of exultation therefore, that he hailed the circumstances, already narrated, by which I had become her husband. Still, I do not mean to say that he counselled, encouraged, or in any wise contributed to those arrangements of his brother, by which that event was precipitated. Let me do him the justice to say, that I verily believe the event, as it did happen, was distasteful to him. His simple wish, as he frankly avowed to me afterwards, was that we should grow together, by the natural tendencies of a sympathetic passion, and he did not believe that his brother would seriously oppose my departure from their retreat, when my connection with Helen should become indissoluble. He did not know the despotical nature of that man. He did not conceive it possible that such a connection, as that which Bud Halsey acknowledged with the outlaws, could so completely subdue and set at nought, the natural ties of kindred flesh and blood. He was yet to learn, how terribly and entirely this was to be done hereafter.

It will be easy to understand how, even to him, not less than my wife, the idea that I was about to be beguiled from my virtue, by the subtleties of Mowbray, was of intolerable annoyance. He had indulged himself in the hope, that I was to restore his daughter to society. For himself he had no serious cares on this subject. He, too, would like to return to society. He lived among the outlaws in a sort of Coventry, distrusting them, and half distrusted by them;—but he was no longer so youthful as to feel deeply the privation, except on account of one, whose happiness was truly so much dearer than his own. He did not doubt that the time would come, when I should be suffered to go free, and he shrunk with horror from the thought that, meanwhile, I should be guilty of any course of conduct, which should lessen my desire to return, or affect my peace of mind and security when I did so. The changes in my deportment surprised him, and, as in the case of his daughter, at the first blush, gave him pleasure. They had both been disposed to ascribe my previous gloom to a lessening of my regard for the latter—to the staling of a boyish passion in possession of its object; and a change in this respect, in my conduct, was too grateful at first sight, to render them at all desirous of seeking farther into its causes. But when my intimacy with Mowbray was remarked—when, too, it was seen that I betrayed more curiosity—more sympathy—with the proceedings of the outlaws,—and when Bud Halsey began to regard me with favor;—every apprehension of poor Helen was aroused. The favor of her uncle, seemed to her, one of the most doubtful and dangerous of signs. The danger seemed conclusive, when, one morning, Bud Halsey sent me my horse. The brave animal had been taken from me, at my first coming—I had not been permitted to see him since, and when, with a sentiment of pride and pleasure which I could not conceal, I went forth, laid my hand upon his neck, and heard him whinny his recognition as he heard my voice,—then all her suspicions seems confirmed. I was about to leap upon him, with all that gush of unmeasured exultation, which youth feels, confident of strength, buoyant with prospects of assured success, and in the possession of one of those agents of power and speed, in the employment of which the impetuous nature feels all that enthusiasm and delight which grows out of the intimate union and joint action of blood and brain;—my hand was on his neck, my foot in the stirrup—when Helen called me to her side.

"Go not yet, dear Henry—come with me first—but a moment. I would speak with you."

I confess to a little reluctance at quitting the animal, even at the solicitation of one so dear. But I followed her. There was nobody besides in the cottage. Her father had gone out on a ramble. When I joined her in the chamber to which she had returned, she at once, and passionately, putting her hand upon my arm, thus addressed me:—

"Oh, Henry, forgive me, but I fear you, I suspect you!"

"Suspect me?—of what, dear Helen?"

"This horse, this new favor of my uncle, your intimacy with that Mr. Mowbray, all make me tremble lest they seduce you to their evil practices —lest you should be tempted,—lest you should fall! Oh, Henry, be not tempted, be firm, go not with them to do evil. Go not,—for my sake, Henry, for your own sake;—go not, go not!"

I kissed her, oh! how fondly—pressed her to my bosom—and while the tears gathered in her eyes,—while she clung to me with continued pleading,—I begged her to be quiet—to believe me still. It was necessary, however, that I should maintain appearances, and, breaking from her, I hurried to horse, and proceeded to join Mowbray in a canter which he proposed. How I felt myself, once more on horseback! What a feeling of pride it inspires, mounted on a noble steed who knows his own strength, and rejoices in the free play of his majestic limbs. My horse knew his rider, and I him, and as I rode forth to meet Mowbray, I found myself calculating the chances of a long chase, through swamp and through briar, against any, the best mettled, in the camp of the outlaws.

CHAPTER EIGHTEEN

It will be unnecessary that I should enter into the details of the game which I had taken it in hand to play. Of the numerous daily interviews I had with Mowbray, and others of the outlaws, I shall say little. Let it suffice that I flattered myself with having fooled them all to the top of their bent. Even Bud Halsey, I at length grew satisfied, had become convinced that I was ready to thrust out my cold iron, and cry 'stand!' to a true man, whenever he should give the signal. In this, the probabilities favored me. It was natural enough that a youth of my age and temper, situated as I was at the moment, should soon overcome the scruples of my education, in an anxiety to feel my freedom once more—nay, that my principles should very soon become corrupted, breathing such a rogues' atmosphere, and in daily contact with some of the choicest specimens of scroundrelism. I had striven, in playing my part, not to suffer it to appear that I made the transition too easily from a rugged honesty to loose indifference to all its exactions. On the contrary, at first, I allowed it to appear that my chief pleasure was in being once more on horseback. I next suffered Mowbray to perceive that his conversation interested me. I laughed heartily at his jests;—he had no small powers of humor, and could hit off a ludicrous picture in low life with the extravagance and felicity of Lover. By little and little I let myself be led to association with others, and, finally, to partake in their amusements. The outlaws were generally great cardplayers, and Mowbray himself was an adept. They had other amusements, some of which were even of less intellectual character. Quoits, hurling the bar, and the Indian ball-play, were in common use, at moments of leisure;—and, for the indulgence of these amusements, they had more than one fine amphitheatre, formed by natural but small prairie spots in the Swamp. Pistol and rifle shooting, I readily joined in, for reasons that will be understood. It gave me practice in the weapons upon which, could I secure them, it might be that I should have to depend;—though, when I saw how expert were the outlaws generally with them, I shuddered at the idea of encountering them. I have seen them frequently trim their dog's ears and tails by rifled-pistols, at ten or twelve paces; and there was one of them, an Alabamian, by the name of Brewton, that could, at every shot, hit a half dollar piece while falling, which he himself had thrown into the air. I could do nothing like this, but I could lay my bullet at twelve paces within the circle of a man's breast, and I did not care, for such purposes as I had in view, to do better than that.

In these sports, Bud Halsey now frequently joined us, and, if you can suppose such a thing as civility in a bear, then was he civil to me. He had a sort of rough, condescending pleasantry about him, when in a good humor, which greatly increased his popularity with the men, but which, as it was a seeming condescension, was more offensive to my pride than had been his insolence and harshness. But I contrived to keep down my gorge, and to stomach, in some way, what I could not easily digest. It was a severe task, but I toiled faithfully to maintain appearances suited to the new character I had assumed. I pleased myself with the hope that I had deceived him. He evidently looked with satisfaction at my increasing familiarity with his men, and at my engaging in practices which, if not in themselves immoral, are at least very often associated, among men, with those which are so. I gamed, and drank, and swore—growing worse, every day, by little and little, and reconciling myself to these excesses by a frequent secret reference to the object which I desired to attain. It was a gratifying thing to me, as it convinced me of my successful acting, that Bush Halsey and his daughter both appeared to take my change of character seriously to heart. At length, her frequent sighs changed to expostulations, and it became a task of greater difficulty than ever to keep my secret. I could only evade and baffle scrutiny by putting on an air of levity and recklessness, which usually had the effect of silencing the entreaties which I felt that it might be imprudent to satisfy.

But my change of demeanor and profession, involved me in one difficulty, extrication from which was not so easy. Having given a loose on one occasion, to my new principles, and very deliberately declared my scorn of the social contract as it existed in legalized society, in the hearing of Mowbray, I was confounded by his clapping me on the shoulder and telling me that a fine chance was now before me for making a beginning—that Bud Halsey had received intelligence of a large sum of government money being on its way from one of the land-offices, which it was his design to make sure of, and, for this purpose, meant to scatter his whole force, in every direction along the possible route of travel. Bud Halsey

made his appearance suddenly, a moment after, and confirmed the statement. I fancied I could detect a keenness of glance, an intense and
searching expression in his eye, as he listened for what I should say. I did
not hesitate. I professed myself pleased with an occasion to try my skill,
concluding with the hope that the affair might be a spirited one—that the
guardian of the money would find an occasion of fight.

"If you have the stomach for it," said Bud Halsey, "you shall be the first
at the gripe. But you are scarcely the man," said he, with something of a
sneer, "for such a business. You have not been long enough from your
mother."

"You shall see!" I replied, though I did not exactly see the purpose of
his sneer, unless it was to goad my vanity.

The movement promised to be an important one with me. What did
I propose to do? What did I promise myself by it? It was not until after I
was committed to the enterprise that I asked myself this question. Then,
the whole results opened before my eyes. What should I aim at but escape?
I should be provided with horse and weapons—and a sudden dash to right
or left would be only a natural movement such as was to be expected from
the events of such an expedition. On the other hand, there was the danger
of being suspected, and sped by an expeditious bullet; or of not being able
to carry through my decision of escape from the lack of opportunity, and
of being compelled to countenance, if not assist in the contemplated
robbery. The affair was no child's play, and it behoved me to consider it
with equal calm and resolution. I had gone too far to recede. Beside, the
confinement to which I was subjected had become so irksome that I was
willing to encounter any risk rather than continue in it. As it promised to
be unending otherwise, I felt that the earliest movement was necessarily
the best. I said nothing of my design, however, to my wife. I preferred that
she should neither hear nor suspect it, till I was off. Is it asked whether I
proposed to abandon her? Far from it. I truly loved her,—but I could not
bear the torment of my situation, and my purpose was to leave a letter for
her, declaring my feelings, the necessity by which I was impelled, and my
wish that she should rejoin me at an early moment in Alabama. I designated a spot where I would meet her, and pacified my own doubts with the
conviction that once I had fairly escaped from his clutches, there could
be no motive on the part of Bud Halsey, to keep his niece from a situation in life, in which, while he could fear no risk, she would hold an agreeable and honorable station. But I did not know the man.

CHAPTER NINETEEN

My determination was not suffered to remain a secret. The day previous to our contemplated foray, Bush Halsey, my wife's father, returned to the cottage in no little excitement. His daughter and myself were sitting beside the fire. His countenance was filled with an agitation which he did not endeavor to conceal; and, after a hurried glance about the premises to see that there were no eaves-droppers, he addressed me, in my wife's hearing, after the following manner:

"Henry, what's this that Bud Halsey tells me? He says that you go forth with him, to-morrow night—I need not say on what sort of business."

"It is even so, Sir."

"Henry, dear Henry!" exclaimed Helen, approaching me, confounded, incapable of saying more, yet saying, how much, in that brief, broken exclamation.

"You cannot mean it!" said the father.

"What am I to do, Sir?" I asked—"remain here all my life—doomed —a vegetable forever?"

"Do not this, at least! Better remain the vegetable. Incur not that terrible destiny of my brother, in which, though free from his crimes, I must still partake. For God's sake, young man, think of your parents, friends, rank in society—reputation! Think! think!"

I need not detail the conversation. The reader will perceive its tone. The agonized entreaties of my wife,—the earnest, pleading exhortations of her father—his tears no less than hers—assuring me of their joint sincerity— left me without any good reason why I should not relieve them from their sufferings, by letting them know the whole truth. I told my story—showed how I had been practising upon Mowbray and his fellows—and what was the particular motive of my present determination.

"It is perilous, but I cannot disapprove of your plan. Go when you will, it will, perhaps, be inevitable that you should incur some risk. I too, have been thinking of this flight,—not for myself—for there is nothing to be gained by me, in going once more into a gentler world,—but for you and Helen. Why not work together now? We shall, perhaps, never have a better chance if we wait a thousand years."

My wife eagerly caught at the idea. I was not less pleased with it myself; but was less sanguine of success in an attempt at escape, burdened with a woman, under circumstances that would require great promptness, and possibly involve the necessity of fighting. But Bush Halsey met all my objections.

"I have been somewhat prepared for such a movement, for some weeks past. I saw your unhappiness for a time, and readily understood it. It was then that I planned a mode of operations, of which I should have spoken to you before, but for the sudden change in your behavior—a change only to be accounted for, by supposing that you had become completely reconciled to your bonds, and, which was worse, not less reconciled to the loose morals by which they were governed. Now that we understand one another, we can act together, and with a better prospect of success. Let me tell you my plan."

Bush Halsey had indeed taken up the affair with a degree of energy, quite unusual with him. He surprised me, not less by his activity and progress, than by the plausibleness of his scheme. After giving me the details, he proceeded thus:

"The two plans can be made to harmonize admirably. The boat lies on Cedar Island—the creek broadens at that point with a swift current, and carries us, without effort, into the main stream. Once let us pass Buffalo Bend, and we are pretty safe. That is the last point of land on which Bud keeps a watch. The difficulty will be in getting to the boat on Cedar Island. Cedar Island is two miles off. The route is circuitous and well watched. But the watch will be diminished when Bud Halsey takes the road, and you have, to a certain extent, disarmed suspicion. Now, this is what I propose. Bud sets off at sundown—you are to follow with Mowbray, Hard-Riding Ross, and a couple more, who are, in reality, but spies upon you. They will call for you at dark. Your horse shall be in waiting for you at the front door, and everything shall look as if you were getting yourself in readiness within. Meanwhile, you shall garb yourself in my old grey overcoat. My slouch-cap will pretty well cover your brows and hair. Your height is very nearly that of mine, your bulk is something less, but we have no moon, and, even with a bright starlight down upon you, the difference between our persons is not so great, as to startle the suspicions of any of our fellows. You shall take my staff, imitate my walk, and find your way down through the pine avenue, along the main trace, which you can keep with tolerable ease, if there be any light at all. There will be three sentries at most, whom you will meet—possibly but one,—and as I have been pursuing this very walk for three weeks past, now giving the word, but most frequently not even accosted, the probability is that you will pass securely in like manner. You will find Helen already at the boat. She must contrive to get there by another route, a full hour before you. As soon as you join her, let the canoe drop with the stream, until you get to Fawn's Point—she knows the place —there you will run into a cove, and at that place, I must join you. You could scarcely get along into, and down the river, unless with a pilot. It is fortunate that I am a good one.—Meanwhile, I will keep Mowbray and his dogs in play, until I think you safe on the water, and then get to you as I can. He will probably send or ride after Bud Halsey, to advise him of your flight. He will scarcely think to impede mine."

Much more was said, which it is not necessary to repeat. But we perfected our arrangements quite as satisfactorily as it was in the nature of circumstances to allow. Meanwhile, the task of dissimulation was doubly difficult. That night I took supper with Mowbray, had a famous *rouse* of it, and listened, for the tenth time, to one of his most licentious stories.

CHAPTER TWENTY

The next day dawned upon us fair and light. The better to disarm suspicion, I spent the morning in company with Mowbray, and in exercise on horseback. I dined at the cottage,—Bud Halsey looking in just before my arrival, and asking where I was. I met him when leaving Mowbray, after our morning's ride. He gave me a smile of peculiar significance, but said nothing. I remembered this smile afterwards, when it became a question with me whether I had ever, for a single moment, succeeded in deceiving this keen-sighted and suspicious outlaw. Our dinner passed in silence. I had no appetite. Helen's eyes were tearful. Bush Halsey was in better spirits, though his mood seldom rose above that evening serene which had always marked his calm, benevolent disposition. Dinner was scarcely over before Helen prepared to take her departure. She was to seek the island by a route at once unpleasant and circuitous. It was necessary that we should not all be seen on the same route. That which I was to take, was assigned me, as the easiest to be found by one so much a stranger as myself to the intricacies of the Swamp. We parted with many tears, as if we were never to meet again;—but she was firm, though she wept. When she was gone, the old man and myself went once more through our calculations. Every step we were to take was to be precisely understood by both. This done, I rode to Mowbray's. I had two objects in this visit. I wished, in the first place, to be seen up to the latest moment preceding my flight; and I was also desirous of securing the pistols with which I had been practicing. It seemed to be reasonable enough that, on the eve of starting on a perilous expedition, I should demand the weapons which a stubborn cashier might render necessary. Nothing of moment transpired during this visit. The Swamp was everywhere astir. Steeds stood here and there, saddled beneath the tree, waiting the rider and the word; and there was an air of general preparation over the encampment, which was equally picturesque and pleasing.

I got the pistols without difficulty, and, hallooing to me on leaving him, Mowbray reminded me to be in readiness at dark. I did not need his warning. I was very soon ready for the worst. Evening seemed very slow of approach, and when twilight had fallen, which it did at that season, and in that situation, in an instant, I still felt that there was quite too much light. But I dismissed my nervous doubts and made ready. The old grey cloak, the slouch cap, the white cotton neck handkerchief, were soon huddled on, and, with my pistols in my bosom, and a good, stout, silver-headed hickory in my grasp, I went forth, as a hale, heavy man of fifty, with just a slight stiffness in my lower limbs. Fortune favored me. I reached the canoe in safety, and found poor Helen half dead with apprehension. My coming filled her equally with tears and strength. She grasped the paddle with as much dexterity as an Indian maiden would have done, and as much grace as a princess. Slight and beautiful, she was yet a creature of great resolve, when the moment came of great necessity. This is a striking character-istic of our Southern women, as known from the earliest pages of our history. Delicate and feeble as it would seem in make, languid and luxu-rious in disposition, they will yet, when aroused by the pressure of extreme events, sudden danger, and painful necessities, meet the crisis with the souls of men—with souls, in some respects, very far superior, indeed, to those of the most heroic men. Men struggle with the consciousness of strength, but the struggles of women are undertaken with an opposite conviction. It is with a full knowledge of their weakness that they come to the encounter with those evils, to meet which seems to demand the utmost exercise of strength.

On we went! Our paddles were scarcely needed. We swept down with the current as fast as we desired, probably at the rate of four miles an hour. The stars gave us abundant light. The silence of night was upon us—how solemnly. Not a whisper broke from our lips, but, shifting with the stream, and only plying the paddle to keep us from the banks, our little boat went onward like a spiritual thing, hardly making a ripple on the bosom of the water. Thus we wound, to and fro, in and out, in a progress that, however rapid, did not, in half an hour, carry us far from our starting place. Such was the circuitousness of the creek. At length, Helen broke the silence with a whisper. Bending forward, she said:—

"Here, Henry,—this is Fawn's Point, where father said we must stop. The cove is on the other side, where we are to wait for him."

Our paddles dipped simultaneously, and, slightly changing her direc-tion, the canoe rounded into as beautiful a little cove, as ever harbored the shallop of a Choctaw princess. We run her up beneath some clustering bays, and, without making fast, we waited in silence for the signal of Bush Halsey. I never passed a more tedious two hours in my life. More than once I proposed to Helen to proceed.

"Your father is safe," I said,—"he has nothing to fear. It is probable he finds it impossible to reach us. We can get on without him."

She objected, insisting that, as I knew nothing of the route, I must lose my way, and probably fall again into the meshes of confederacy. There was reason in the objection. To fall again into their hands, after an effort to escape, would have been a certain death. But delay was dreadfully oppressive. We were not able to converse for fear of alarming some unfriendly ears. We could not move about for fear of disturbing some unfriendly watch, but, crouching in the dark, we lay cramped up in our little dug-out, in a situation of constraint and impatience that would have been utterly intolerable, except that Helen was lying in my arms. More than once, while in this situation, we heard noises, or fancied them. The bushes would stir, possible as some wild beast pushed through them, some bear or deer—the dried leaves would crackle as beneath the crushing tread of some slow, heavy person or animal; and my keen, and, just now, suspicious ears, caught up sounds that I could scarcely satisfy myself, or Helen, did not fall from the lips of some whispering watcher.

At length we heard a distinct alarm throughout the Swamp. It must be remembered, though we had taken so long a time in reaching it, that we were then only about half a mile, by an air line, from our little cottage settlement. A bugle was thrice heard to sound,—followed by the cry of a dozen beagles, faintly swelling upon the breeze, or struggling into echoes from every quarter.

"The alarm!" said Helen, starting from my embrace. "They are on the chase. The beagles are in cry."

"Shall I not put off now?" I demanded.

"No! O no! We are in the dark here. Let us wait."

The sounds dies away, and half an hour more elapsed, without any other alarm, except in a single instance, when, it seemed to us, as if a beagle gave tongue not two hundred yards from us, seemingly just on the other side of the creek. At length a faint rustle was heard,—not more distinct than had reached us before; and, when we least expected him, Bush Halsey stole through the copse under the shadow of which we lay. Pushing off as he stepped into our little vessel, he whispered:

"We are pursued, closely I fear, and possibly watched. I expected to have been overtaken. Why I have not been, I know not. They were ahead of me at one time, and Bud Halsey himself upon the trail."

The words struck me with instant apprehension. His own approach had been made with so little noise, and I had heard quite as much before his coming, that I began to be filled with surmises and misgivings. But not a word was said. In another moment we were out of the cove, and began to feel the full power of the current. Suddenly a voice hailed us from the point of land to which we were nearing.

"Boat!"

A thunderbolt would not have more astounded us, falling at our feet in the calm of a winter day.

"Boat!" the cry was repeated from the very island we had left. "Pull in or we fire!" We now understood the whole. The pursuers had scattered themselves along the head lands. Having an intimate knowledge of the route, they had reached the several points before Bush Halsey, who had been greatly delayed in his progress to join us by the active interference of his brother;—and that brother was on our heels! We had every thing to fear. Again the summons, and the distinct clicking of the gun-lock was significant of the coolest determination. Bush Halsey reached forward and pulled Helen down in the boat towards him. I was on the forward seat. Not a word was spoken, and our paddles dipped the water simultaneously and with the strength of sinews braced to their utmost tension by the necessity and danger. A voice, stern, keen, superior struck our ears—a voice that we too well knew.

"Bush Halsey, be not a fool! You cannot pass, and by God! if you try it we shoot. I mean it. You know me! The treachery of my own brother is his death."

We were visible enough, not as individuals, but as a whole. The boat, like some dark animal, was gliding through the water. We were rapidly passing our enemies. Bush Halsey whispered me:—

"But a few yards will save us. That point, if we round it, will give us shelter. A stout pull,—now."

A shot whistled before me—perhaps, meant as a warning,—an exhortation to provoke no farther the wrath of him by whom we were threatened. At the sound, Helen started up in terror, and stretched her hands towards me, and, simultaneously with this movement, we received a volley. I felt a slight pricking sensation in my left arm, but forgot it all, as a half-suppressed scream from Helen betrayed either her apprehensions or her hurt. We rounded the point at the same instant, and were thus safe for the moment from our enemies. I turned to Helen, who lay, as before, backward, in the arms of her father.

"Helen!" I said, with a tear, which I could not subdue, "Helen!"

She answered with a moan.

"Helen!" said the father, huskily, as he listened. "Helen, my child, you are not hurt."

"I am,—father—Henry."

"God!—it is not—cannot be true."

She sank the next instant, with limbs relaxed and nerveless, down into the bottom of the boat. Bush Halsey and myself turned to her at the same moment. She had swooned—we sprinkled her with water, but we could do nothing for her where we were. While we busied ourselves about her, the boat grounded. We lay on a muddy ledge, which skirted an island thickly set with fresh trees.

"It is well, Henry. We can take her ashore here. I know the place. I think we are safe."

We landed in silence, the old man persisting in bearing Helen on his own shoulder to the shore. She had come out of her swoon, and now and then she moaned, and strove to speak.

CHAPTER TWENTY-ONE

We were very soon able to read her destiny. We carried her on shore to die! Her career of youth and happiness was short indeed. The shot was in her breast and fatal. We spread a couch for her of leaves and bushes, beneath the shelter of a close copse of evergreens, and covered her with the grey overcoat which had disguised me in my flight. We did not need to tell her that we had no hope. She felt by certain instincts that we should have none.

"Henry, I am dying," she said to me, as her father wandered off. I know not what I said in reply;—something, perhaps, which I meant to be consolatory,—some one of those idle common-places, in which the bystander would deceive others, when he cannot deceive himself.

"No!" she continued; "I have no hope but that we shall meet again. That is my hope and my prayer. Oh! my Henry, pray for it,—pray for me! It is not so hard to die with such a hope,—but I fear, Henry, I tremble. I am not, I have not been good enough to die—I loved the world too much —I loved you too much, Henry. God forgive me,—but was not this the punishment. It was a short-lived rapture, my Henry,—Oh! how very short!"

I buried my face in the leaves. I could not speak—nay, I could not weep. The fountain of tears seemed utterly dry. The old man returned and kneeled beside her with me. She was sinking into stupor, with occasional awakenings—awakenings of a higher and more spiritual life. She spoke of things, to us, as it seemed, wildly, but no doubt they had meaning for finer senses. How slowly, how sadly went that night away. It was a pure and gentle night—blessed with many stars, that kept trooping overhead in noiseless march, and looking down stealthily above us with their strange sad eyes. There was a slight breeze, that swayed the trees around us with a not unpleasant and spiritual murmur; and the chafing of the creek upon the little dark beach, along whose slippery edges we had struggled with our precious burthen, mingled a most unseemly but faint music with the strain. I remained close beside her all the night, but she ceased after awhile to be conscious of my presence. She had sunk into a condition something like sleep. Towards daylight she roused herself.

"Where are you, Henry? I see you not. I feel much better,—but I do not see you. Come to me."

"I am here, dear Helen."

"Why do I not see you, then?"

"Your hands are in mine—it is my lip that is pressing on your cheek."

"Something is over my eyes—father,—Henry—take the cloak from my face that I may see you. I am better now!"

And so speaking she died! I do think she was better then—better then, and blessed! She was certainly with God!

CHAPTER TWENTY-TWO

Coldly the day dawned upon us, and with an aspect of peculiar desolation. The inanimate form of Helen was still clasped in my close embrace. The old man spoke.

"We are alone, my son! We are alone."

Oh! how true, how touching were his words. What a change had the morning brought us—what a change from day to night. But a few hours ago, and I was all buoyancy—nay, in the impetuosity of my mood,—in my eagerness to escape from the duresse in which I was detained, had I not calmly contemplated flight, leaving it to a doubtful chance whether I should ever meet with her again. Now it was very certain that we were separated—separated forever in life, and O! how completely,—I could not well comprehend how life was to be sustained! She had become a part of my life; torn from me, I began to realize the vague sensations of a heart from which certain vital sources of pulsation are suddenly withdrawn. Such a chill as remains—such a tremulous uncertainty of sensation. But one seldom dreams long over the dead. Death is among the most certain of the things of life. It is no illusion. It is a terrible reality. Its touch palsies,—its aspect chills—its stony glare rebukes, and mocks, and warns. Icy lips—I pressed them—but it was with the feeling of one who sought for pain and mortification. Stony eyes! I gazed in them, as one would gaze within his own allotted sepulchre. The future as well as the past, lay before me in the present. The unforgotten past, the undeveloped future. Awful volume!—my heart was too full to read it. I shrunk from its dreary, dreamy lessons in dismay. I shrunk into myself—into my own littleness; and, assured of the great loss which I had just sustained, remembered with a glow of shame, upon what small game my previous thoughts had been set. How mean and petty were the objects of my eager thirst. How contracted, limited and worthless the poor things of the finite upon which I had set

my heart. What a precious thing is the love of a pure heart, when it is lost
to us forever!

But what were my woes to his, that desolate old father? What are the
sorrows of youth, at the worst, to those of age? Youth has so many
resources in youth itself. The soul is still active and impetuous—the blood
still ready for new encounters, nay, desiring them; and every pulse and
emotion vibrates with a vitality which soon provides recompense for every
failure and mortification. The heart still sends forth new tendrils in place
of those which have been lopt away, or are withered, and it is seldom
indeed that they do not attach themselves to other objects, in the absence
of the lost, which partly, or perhaps wholly, supply their deficiencies. But
the heart of the old man, like the aged plant, has no such resources—puts
forth no new tendrils. Rend the branches—sunder the close clinging
stems, and the hurt penetrates to the core, and fixes there. The worm
follows and decay. The heart is eaten out and gone, though a few fresh
leaves, a little coronal of green, may yet be seen upon its mossy top, in sign
rather of the immortal principle of life than of the tree that lived. The
saddest sight in nature is that of age tottering to the grave, unsupported
by the dutiful arms of youth. How sterile is such a life—lingering on after
the loss of the beloved ones—looking on their tombs, and until it forgets
its own. I thought, even at that moment, of these things, as I thought of
Helen's father. And yet, he looked upon the inanimate form with a strange
and most unnatural calmness. He had loved her with a love surpassing the
love of woman. He had lost her, at the moment when such a loss was least
to be feared;—and, by what a sudden stroke! It may be he was stunned—
that, like myself, he did not realise our privation so completely as I, at least,
was yet destined to to. But no! his eye was filled with as much intelligence
as calm. Whence did he derive a consolation, of which I had nothing? I
have not said before that he was a religious man—prayerful, truly devout.
Such an assurance may amuse the thoughtless. Piety in the abode of
outlaws! Prayer, religion, where the hourly practice is crime! But, it was
nevertheless true. Bush Halsey was a weak man—it was an error in him to
continue in the Swamp, witnessing what he had not power to prevent,—
but his instincts were just—his heart was in the right place, and he kept his
hands clean from the sins in which all around him, but his dear child,
wallowed freely. At this hour, struggling, as he did, against his loss, the calm
upon his face was no bad sign of that within his soul. It was the calm
derived from resignation —a calm which nothing else can give; and, sitting
beside the body of the beloved, he at the foot, and I supporting the
precious head, with all its weight of drooping ringlets—he conversed of

death—its mystery—its sublimity—its repose. Philosophy, in its cold and questioning mood, would have mocked at such discourse as that in which we dwelt. It was either beyond or below philosophy,—for, in our belief of the spiritual world, we were both children. But the philosophy of the worldling will never bring to any definite knowledge on the subject either of death or life. Its beginning and ending recognizes these conditions, but nothing more. The teaching which can influence us any farther, must be addressed to the heart—to that faith which seems to me equally born of our instincts and some blessed sympathetic influence which favors our aspiration and wishes from without. I believe, if we are earnest in the call, we may evoke spirits now, as in those days when angels walked among men. They walk among us now, as they did in the days of the patriarch:—

"Good spirits are beside us night and day!"

Good spirits *are* beside us. Helen, Oh! Helen, wert thou not beside us, on that day, when thy freed spirit—violently freed—regained its first life, but hung, hovering, on suspended wing, and sanctified to our souls the precious hour that followed! Else, how was it that, lonely as we were, there was such a flood of serenity around us! Thou wert with us, my Helen—thy spirit was upon the scene, and in our hearts,—and the skies smiled though we were sad,—and we both felt, that in love we were not unremembered, and that if God had ravished the blessed spirit from the frail tabernacle in which it had first found its dwelling, it had not been entirely taken from the world of which we were a part. We still breathed an atmosphere in which floated ever the pure soul of the creature whom we loved.

"My son," said the old man,—"Henry!—you must leave this place. It is not for you a place of safety. It is for her. It will be for me. But you will be pursued. You must contrive your flight this very day."

"What mean you, Sir? Am I to go alone? Do you not go with me,—and these precious remains—shall they not go with us until we can find consecrated ground?"

"All earth is consecrated ground. God had made it all. The uses to which we put the earth consecrates it. What place of city sepulchre is more pure than this? The islet is very lovely to the eye. Trees and shrubs keep it ever green. The waters which bathe it on every side, keep it ever pure. Birds live here and sing throughout the year. Man does not vex the spot with his strifes and follies. Can there be a fitter place for the grave of my child, who was so pure and so lovely? No, Henry—it is here that we must make her grave."

We searched out a spot for the purpose. The island was generally a flat, but in the centre there was a slight elevation, crowned by a clump of gigantic cotton-wood trees. The shade was equally sweet and sepulchral. There was a copse of thick vines and shrubs which partially enclosed it, and which we knew would be covered in the spring with the honeysuckle, the jessamine, and other sweet-scented flowers. Here then we brought her. Here, with the paddles of our canoe, we scooped out a narrow grave, and making a bed of leaves, we wrapped her in the thick grey close-bodied coat of her father, and laid her down to her eternal rest. Sweet form, so dear to me, shut in forever from my sight! Sweet spirit, so blessing, still hovering around my own!—my only prayers were my pangs. I could not shovel in the earth upon her—I did not—the old man did it all. How could I cast the earth upon the white unprotected limbs, which, but a few hours ago, had embraced me with a passion so tender and so true.

We sat beside her grave for hours after, but with little speech from either. What was spoken related to the solemn subjects upon which the old man had already spoken—life and death! These are the great engrossing subjects. Strange! how people strive to evade them. How the shudder which follows the first thought of death, makes them recoil from the second, as if it were a subject which we might put by at will—as if it were not, in fact, the only thing in life which is inevitable. The first shudder over, the thought of death is morally wholesome. We should think of it daily, not only of its inevitability, but as of a thing, the character of which is to be mainly influenced by our daily actions. Could we think thus, religion were easy—it were the next step in the simple process of bringing back the stray sheep to the Good Shepherd.

CHAPTER TWENTY-THREE

It was sunset. To this hour we had lingered by the little hillock, which had shut in from our eyes forever, the thing that was so precious in our sight. I had given myself up to the feeling of desolation which took possession of me. I lay beside the grave, my fingers penetrated the soft mould, which was soon to become enriched by hers. My brow lay upon the damp earth. A sort of stupor seemed to overcome me. But the voice of the old man aroused me to my duties.

"Henry, my son! It is time to depart. Farther delay may endanger your safety. Come! It needs not that we should remain above the grave to mourn. The sorrow of the living attends him and cannot be shut out. Happy, indeed, are we,—did we but know it—that this is the case. How soon would be the feeling of our griefs, did we not strive so recklessly to get rid of them, bring us that perfect peace of the regenerated soul, brought home to God, which we all so much require. We must go, my son—*you* will not forget!"

"Forget, my father,—no! She was too precious for that. Never! Never!"

"Yet the memory of the perished dear one should be a sweet, not a distressing memory. It should strengthen our hearts, while it subdues our passions. Suffering is meant for this. We should grow strong in the prosecution of those duties which are set for us as tasks—duties whether of endurance or of performance,—the reward of which, when done, is life eternal in communion with the beloved ones! Fortunately for me, my son, the duties before me are not of long duration. I shall soon meet with my innocent child. I shall see her first!"

We took our way to the boat in silence. There we found a basket which Helen had brought with her, and which I had not seen before. The provident girl had filled it with cakes, which she had prepared against our journey. We had not eaten all the day,—for that matter, I had scarcely eaten anything

the day before. I had no appetite. I could not partake of the cakes of Helen
—nay, the basket in my eyes gave me a painful feeling. I thought of her
thoughts, her hopes and feelings, as she prepared these little necessaries!—
how sweet would have been our feast together, gliding down, night and
noon-day, along that lonely river. Now! Oh! that now!—I pushed the
basket from my sight.

The old man knew the river well. We glided by *raft* and *snag* and *sawyer*
in perfect safety. Night came on, and we were once more silent voyagers by
the dim light of the stars,—those ever-twiring ministers of night, those
numerous herds of eyes, that spread themselves out or shrink and cover
themselves within her cloudy fold, at the slightest symptoms of her anger.
I leaned back and watched them, and wept silently beneath their glance.
How much is the love of the young heart associated with, and awakened
by, those uncertain periods of time, when twilight, the moon or the stars,
are in the ascendant. The affections do not seem to flourish in the noon-
day. There is something in the intense passionateness of the sun's glare,
that seems to offend the delicacy of youthful sentiment. But the fainter
light, the subdued beauties of evening and night, the pale, insinuating
charms of moon and stars,—win their way to the young affections, without startling, and link themselves to all their dearest emotions. Looking up
to those bright, pale watchers, I could not well believe that I was alone. I
sometimes fancied that two of them, looking more like eyes than stars,
drew nigher to me; and, at such moments, the breeze, which came from
the woods along the waters, seemed to whisper in the very accents of a
beloved one. I was young,—I could still dream—but that poor old man—
who still plied his paddle, now right and now left, with a vigor of stroke
that was really wonderful—he had long since ceased to dream!

I offered to relieve him of his labor, but he would not. Indeed, as I knew
nothing of the river, and as our dug-out depended for its direction upon
the paddle, not upon the tiller—for it had none—any attempt of mine
would, in all probability, during the night, have ended in mischief. Thus
we went—both silent—both absorbed in thoughts, which, as we mutually
understood them, called for no utterance. Sometimes the silence was
broken by the howl of the wolf, the scream of the eagle, or the melancholy
hooting of the owl, from one or other of the shores between which we
stole, like some fairy vessel. At other times we could catch a moaning
sound from the woods, like the far cry of one in distress, which was yet
only the effect of the wind, rushing in currents through unlooked-for
openings of cane, by which, in some places, the banks were lined—regions
of the bear, presenting at times, along the shore, a dense barrier, fully a mile

in depth. How melancholy sweet are thy numerous voices, oh, solemn and mysterious night!

I slept! How long I know not, but I was wakened by the boat striking against the shore. I started and looked up. The old man was standing on the land, upon which he had already drawn one half of the canoe.

"Where are we, sir?" I asked. "What time is it?"

"It is nearly daylight."

"I have slept, then?"

"Yes,—very soundly! You needed it, my son."

"But you, sir?"

"Ah! I need very little,—old people need less than young. The work of renovation is not so necessary in them."

"Do you know where we are, sir?"

"I think I do; but I may have erred in my calculations, as I was anxious not to go too far. We are, I think, about a mile above Baker's Landing. There is a saw-mill somewhere about, which we shall probably see by daylight. I wait for that, to be certain. Here begin the settlements, and here I propose to leave you."

"How, sir, leave me? Will you not go with me, and live with me—my father, mother, all, will be glad to have you?"

"No! Henry, I return to the Swamp."

"Return! Return to the Swamp?"

"Yes! I have nothing now to take me into the world—much to keep me out of it—and *here!*"

I strove vainly to shake his determination, and finally ceased to attempt it. I could not but think he was right. What had he to do in the world—what was the world to him—or he to it? His world was in the forest, there, with his child. At that moment, I half believed that my world was there also. Certainly, the more I thought of leaving it forever, the more difficult it became to subdue my emotions.

Day at length dawned upon us. The saw-mill was in sight, and a cluster of cabins running down to the very brink of the stream. The old man pointed them out, and taking from his breast a purse of half-eagles, forced it into my hand. I did not scruple at receiving it. I had no money. What I had when I came into the Swamp, had been taken from me, and never returned, when the myrmidons of Bud Halsey took me intocustody.

"With this, Henry, you can easily procure a good horse at any of the settlements along the river—most probably at this. There, God bless you, my son—go—go, and be happy!"

We parted—good old man—but not without a hope,—and not forever!

CHAPTER TWENTY-FOUR

I soon found my way to the saw-mill settlement, where I accounted for my appearance by representing myself as left by a raft, having wandered off from one of the landings into the Swamp. The story was plausible enough, and occasioned no remark. I had rather more difficulty in getting a horse than Bush Halsey had imagined, and was content to take an old hack at forty dollars, being, indeed, the only tolerable animal to be had. I was enough of a jockey to see that the creature had been once badly foundered, nor was this denied by the owner. His hoofs were scaled, and worn low, and he walked tenderly, as if the quick was ailing. But it was Hobson's choice with me, and I did not look closely to his infirmities. I took for granted that he was good for six days travel, and after that he might be crow's meat for what I cared. Paying for him, I found myself with eight half-eagles, and some small change—more than enough to meet my way-side exigencies; and, with a last look upon the river whose contiguous streams had been of such fatal interest to me, I dashed up the narrow Indian trail which, as I was instructed, would conduct me into the main track leading homeward. That day I rode forty miles, and slept at the wigwam of a mulatto, who gave his wife—an Indian woman—a sound drubbing in my very sight, and in spite of all my expostulations. I believe the only offence on her part was that she suffered the fish to burn, which his imperial highness had caught for his own, and which furnished a very sorry portion of my supper. She probably deserved all that she got—was a sulky hag, of fierce, black, revengeful aspect, who, in all probability will have a day of reckoning with him on this very account. My interposition saved her from a part of the flogging—at all events, such was his assurance to me while it was in progress; and with this I had to be satisfied.

The next day I started with the dawn, paying five dollars for my night's lodging, my own, and my horse's supper. I soon discovered, from the lank sides of my horse, that I had paid for him unnecessarily. Yet had I gone into the stable myself, and seen counted out to him thirty good ears of corn;— this too, after he had been nibbling for half an hour on the blades. But the corn had been withdrawn from the trough after I had retired. The poor animal was evidently suffering from starvation. He bore me feebly, and with tottering footsteps. At noon I stopped on the edge of a *field* prairie, where the grass was tolerably good, and continued for an hour to 'chew the cud of sweet and bitter fancy,' while he digested more stable material. This freshened him a little, and at the close of day, I reached the hovel of a Choctaw, who, in answer to my first enquiry, replied:

"Yaow!—hab 'nough co'n—'nough fodder.—Plenty co'n—plenty fodder! Man eat—hoss eat—plenty co'n, 'nough co'n—too much co'n— too much fodder!"

The assurances were thick and substantial, and my Choctaw Boniface promised to be a landlord after the most liberal fashion. He did not misrepresent his corn crib: it was ample. He took me to see it, and then conducted me to his bear-pen, where he had a two-year-old Bruin of the brownest complexion, taming for a pet, which he was very anxious to sell me at seven dollars, to carry home to my squaw. The quizzical chuckle and wink of the good-natured fellow, as he named the squaw, brought the tears into my eyes. He evidently regarded me as a boy who had as yet no thought of a wife. *He* had no wife, but he fondled his bear quite as much as if it were one,—probably much more than he would have fondled the loveliest squaw that he could have found in the whole bosom of his tribe. This fellow did not spare his corn in my case, but gave me an ample supply of bread stuffs for supper,—together with some well broiled slices of smoked venison, of which his cabin had a tolerable supply. He was no doubt an active hunter, when sober. But the signs of whiskey-worship were sufficiently apparent in his face, if not in his cabin. His nose had the sign manual of strong drink, in the largest carbuncles that human nose ever maintained—a congeries of little red hillocks that half reminded me of a settlement of marmozets, or prairie dogs. Unfortunately for me, his liberality in the matter of corn, unlike that of my mulatto host of the night before, was as much shown to my horse as to myself. In looking at the corn crib and the bear, I allowed myself to be diverted from the condition of the animal, and the Indian improvidently gave him his corn and fodder together. The half-starved animal naturally fastened upon the corn and surfeited himself, and when, at dawn, the following morning, I prepared to mount him, I found him dead-foundered, and barely able to walk. Grieved at the event, vexed with myself for my own neglect, I was yet compelled to push forward; and, paying my Choctaw his fare, which called for another of my gold pieces, I set forward—thinking it probable that, as the animal warmed with walking, the stiffness would diminish or disappear. And so it did; but not sufficiently to satisfy me, or relieve my anxiety and impatience; and, after dragging along at the slow pace of three miles an hour, for seven hours, I concluded to abandon the miserable animal, and pursue the rest of my journey, or until I could procure another beast, on foot. There was a slight rising of the country on my left hand, which appeared covered with a pretty thick growth of grass,—and into this I rode him. The woods gave him a very good shelter, and the grass would sustain life until he might be picked up by some traveller or neighbor. At all events, I was resolved not to burden myself any longer with the care of a beast whose limbs could scarcely support his own frame, to say nothing of mine. Ascending the hill, I found a beautiful hollow, where the grass, protected from the sharper winds of winter, was still luxuriant and tender. Here I stripped him, and, after some search, having found a hollow gum of considerable size, I hid away the saddle and bridle, for future use, if necessary. I had scarcely done this, and set the poor creature free, before I heard the tramping of horses from above. Here, then, was a prospect of succor and assistance, much sooner that I could have hoped for it. I hurried immediately towards the road-side, from which I had been removed about an hundred yards, and when I reached the edge of the hill which looked down upon the road,—from which I was effectually screened by a thick undergrowth by which it was edged,—I was about to halloo and spring forward, when a sudden suggestion of prudence persuaded me to stop and first reconnoitre. Accordingly, stooping down, I crawled forward on hands and knees until I reached the edge of the hill, at the foot of which the road ran, and, at this very moment, the travellers whom I had heard drew up below. It was well that I adopted these precautions. The very next moment, my ears were struck by the sounds of a voice which grated harshly upon my ears, as that of my worst enemy. I felt a shuddering horror through my whole frame. Cautiously, I divided the bushes with my hand, and looked below; and there, sure enough, stood Bud Halsey, beside his horse, from which he was about to lift the saddle-bags. His back was to me, but a glance sufficed to show me that he was the man. I involuntarily felt in my breast for my pistols. They were safe. They were well loaded, and my nerves, disquieted for an instant, were again firm. I felt that it would be easy to fell the outlaw in his tracks, and I half resolved—but it was for an instant only—that I would do the deed. But I grew wiser in another moment. In the intenseness of my feelings in regard to this man, I had failed, for the first few minutes, to see that he was not alone. Beside him, dismounting while I gazed, were the *soi distant* parson, Mowbray, and another man, the fellow Warner, of whom I have already spoken, as one whom I remembered to have met before entering the Swamp.

Here was a concatenation accordingly. What was I to do? I could not doubt the intention of these fellows. I could not but believe that their journey was undertaken because of my flight. They were in pursuit of me. That they had no idea of my proximity, I soon felt certain, as they prepared to water the horses and to take refreshments at the spring, which I now perceived to issue from the hill upon which I stood, the water foaming below in a basin several yards in breadth. I was not more than fifteen feet above them, and, at one time, as they were about to seat themselves, I might have so tumbled a rock upon them—had any been convenient— as to have crushed the three. I looked about me, as the thought occurred to me, to see if there was no such friendly fragment at hand.

But, if I had any doubt at first of the object of this journey, it was soon dissipated by the dialogue that ensued between Bud Halsey and Mowbray. There had evidently been a good many previous words between them, for they were both very much irritated. The manner of Mowbray was marked by sullenness, and that of Halsey was fully characteristic of his extremest mood of asperity. The first speaker whose words were distinguishable, was Mowbray,—though the tones of Halsey's voice had reached me as he drew nigh.

"I really never fancied myself a fool, Mr. Halsey, and until it can be shown that I am one,—to blame me for my course in this business is, in fact, in other words, to accuse me of treachery. I see no other alternative."

"And do you suppose, Mr. Mowbray, that, if such a suspicion entered into my head, I should tamely sit here palavering with you? No! no! Sir. By G——d! The stroke would have followed the suspicion, as certainly and soon as the thunder follows the flash. I give few words to traitors, I assure you."

Mowbray muttered something which I could not make out, but the harsh accents of Halsey seemed to drown his utterance.

"I am not in any complimentary mood, and therefore do not call you fool either, as you seem to insist that I do or should. I know that you are no fool, and it is therefore that I blame you. But I will tell you what is the matter with you, Mr. Mowbray—you are a vain man, with all your wisdom, and this boy has flattered your vanity, until he has bedevilled you.

You have ceased to watch him in listening to him. He has seen your weak points, and contriving to make you look inwards, you have been able to see nothing that he has been contriving without. Your vanity, sir,—it is your vanity, sir, that is your weakness—that makes a fool of you, if anything—blinds you at all events to the duties that you take in hand."

"You speak plainly, sir, at all events."

"Ay, ay, it's a trick I have, and as it's plain truth that I generally speak on such occasions, it's not a bad trick. I tell you, Mr. Mowbray, that I have a trick of acting plainly too, upon occasion,—and let me say in your ear, that, when I found how completely you had suffered this chap to slip through your fingers, in a trap of your own making—I found it almost as easy to put a bullet through your ears as to speak to them!"

"I should not have been more a sufferer than by the course you have taken. It is not too late, sir."

"Come, come, Mr. Mowbray,—this will not do. I must have no sulks! You have blundered, shockingly blundered, and I must be permitted my own way of reproaching you for it. The matter is a serious one. It endangers our whole business, our lives and the safety of our men. Let us see that there be no more blundering. This fellow cannot long escape us. He will not, if you do not again suffer that d——d petty weakness of yours, to blind your eyes and baffle your judgment."

Mowbray was silent,—with a silence that betrayed dissatisfaction. The other did not seem to heed it, as he went on:

"By this time every avenue is guarded—every outlet from the Swamp. We must be ahead of him; and, if not, travelling night and day for the next twenty-four hours, will make us so. What sort of a horse was it that he got from that old fool, Houser? Did you think to inquire, Warner?"

"A regular break-down—a poor, foundered spavined critter, not worth skinning. I know the nag well enough. I reckon he's hardly got through the Swamp with him yet."

"And why didn't you follow him when you found out that he was so poorly mounted?" demanded the outlaw.

"You forget, sir, I went down to the mill in the boat. I had no horse, and he had a matter of eight hours start of me."

"Then, be sure, the fellow's dead ahead of us still. He's the chap to push a horse from the jump, without asking how he's to hold out. He's ahead of us, but can't keep so long. At all events we'll push for the 'Raccoon crossing,' and scatter there. We should have him by another sun-rise. D——n him! But for that foolish brother of mine, and the poor girl—

I would that her blood were not upon my hands—poor Helen—any blood but hers!—but for them, all this would have been prevented. We should have had no such trouble. I should never have been so weak—so silly—but it can be mended—at least, it's not too late for that! There shall be no relentings now!"

This was spoken rather in soliloquy. The slight touch of a human nature which the outlaw displayed, when speaking of his niece, brought the tears into my eyes. But his expressions with regard to myself in the next moment dried them, and I could have pistolled him on the spot with a coolness and recklessness not unlike his own.

Their meal was finished in silence. At the abrupt command of their leader, Warner gathered up the fragments, and I saw them mount their steeds, and set off upon the journey, without moving from my position. I caught a glimpse, as they were mounting, of the face of Mowbray, who was the slowest in his movements of the three. I observed that it was almost purple with suppressed choler. He rode after the others in silence, with lips closely compressed, and with the air of a man who could speak daggers, and use them too, if he dared!

CHAPTER TWENTY-FIVE

I felt my heart grow very chill as I reviewed my situation. My path was every where beset, and Bud Halsey, knowing the country as he did, and being the person that he was, was not likely to leave his work unfinished. The conversation of my pursuers was of a kind to leave me hopeless of any escape, except through the merest good fortune, and the most unyielding firmness. On the very path that I was pursuing, my arch enemy, with his two subtle satellites, was himself upon the watch, and yet, I could not choose any other route. I knew of no other, and the very fact that I knew my enemies upon this, who they were and where they were, determined me still to go forward as I had begun. I must take my chance and meet events with whatever courage and conduct I could command. It was evident from what they had said, and from the free rein with which they dashed forward, that there was some certain point ahead, at which they aimed, and where they intended to await me. What was the point? Where was 'Raccoon crossing?' I was ignorant of every step of the route. I had nothing to do but to go forward with as much prudence as possible—to prepare against all sudden surprises—to keep in the cover of the woods, where they were of a nature to suffer me to do so, and to feel my ground at every change of position before betraying myself. In no other way could I hope to avoid the encounter,—for which, should it be unavoidable, I must only man myself with the most desperate resolution. The determination to sell my life as dearly as possible, seemed to nerve me with strength to proceed, and, cutting myself a stout hickory for the wayside, I started forward, with spirits much lighter than seemed to be altogether justified by my situation. A moment's reflection now served to convince me that, what I had lately regarded as a crowning evil—the loss of my horse —was, in reality, somewhat favorable to my hope of escape. It enabled me to keep the cover of the woods, to advance noiselessly, and to conceal myself with more facility on the approach of danger. Encouraged by thoughts like these, and by that sort of audacity which comes from one's desperation, I dashed into motion with a sort of defiance, and, keeping along the margin of the road, ready to seek the shelter of the woods at the smallest alarm, I commenced my pedestrian expedition with all the philosophy of which I was master.

I had always been counted a good *amateur* walker,—but walking as a duty, and in a new, unopened country, following Indian foot-paths, and fording streams, wading swamps, and "*cooning* logs," is a very different business. The road was a terribly broken one, crossed by frequent ravine and rivulet,—for I was not yet entirely out of the Swamp country,—and full of obstructions from fallen trees, vines, briars, stumps, and broken branches. But I was sustained by the very difficulties of my situation. I was stimulated by the trial of my strength, and able to get forward at the rate of three miles an hour, which was probably quite as much as could have been done, in his best days, by the miserable beast I had abandoned. But, five hours at this pace soon lessened pretty equally my strength and elasticity. Towards evening, I began to feel the approaching gravity of the scene. The trees began to cast a longer, denser shadow across my path, and the sun glimmered faintly, sprinkling the open space with a cluster of beaded gold-drops, which, while they caught my glance, and while I looked for them from side to side, did not very much tend to enliven me. The wilderness seldom has its singing birds, and I failed to hear the chirp of one the whole afternoon. Once, a couple of deer glided over the road from one thicket to another, but sign of living thing beside, I saw not; and, as the sun disappeared, a couple of screech owls commenced a most gloomy death-duett, from opposite sides of the path over which I was to make my way, and seemed to accompany my progress for a good half hour after. The moon rose, however, almost with the disappearance of the sun, and I gave her, from the bottom of my heart, a traveller's benison. She poured a steady blaze of light across the path, and thus enabled me to avoid its pitfalls and obstructions. Having no place of retreat, and with my spirits somewhat revived by her countenance, I still pursued my way, resolving to continue on until absolutely worn out with fatigue. For three hours more I did so, but weariness began to wrap me as with a cloud. I staggered rather than walked along the path, and, to keep my eyes open, though I felt no hunger, I took from my pockets one of the corn biscuits with which I had provided myself at the hovel of the Choctaw, and commenced eating against time. While thus engaged, I happened upon a trail which struck into the woods upon my right, and seemed to lead to an opening, which was partially discernable from the road—the moonlight falling down upon the space, in a body, giving it the appearance of a placid lake. My exhaustion furnished me with sufficient reason why I should turn into this path, which I did without a moment's hesitation. I followed it for some hundred and fifty yards, when it forked. I took one of the branches at hazard, followed it some fifty yards farther, and found myself suddenly in front of a rude shanty of logs, more like the den of a wild animal than the dwelling of a human being. Prudence would have counselled me rather to find my night's rest in the thicket than in such a hovel;—but the sight of anything in the shape of human habitation, seemed to me to convey the idea of security. Besides, this place was evidently abandoned, and had been long without a tenant. I did not plunge into it headlong, but exercising all the circumspection that I could command, in that general dulling of the faculties that had been produced by weariness and cold, I examined the hut cautiously from the outside,—taking care to peer into it from each corner,—and without seeing anything to alarm me. The roof, which had been originally a thin thatch of pine boughs and leaves, was half broken in and lay upon the ground below—the ends of the remaining branches still hanging half way down and threatening a further fall. The door which was made of plank, was thrown down within;—and such, in short, was the generally desolate air of the place, that I took possession at once, taking for granted that my pursuers were considerably ahead of me,—and of other persons I had nothing to fear. I was, perhaps, more readily persuaded to give this preference to the hovel over the woods, as, by this time, I could hear, rising at intervals from the deep recesses of the swamp-thickets, confused sounds, not unlike the hoarse voices of beasts of prey preparing to emerge for their nightly orgies. I could not doubt that, among these, the sharp bay of the wolf was a frequent sound;—and, as it would not be prudent for me to raise a fire, lest, in driving the brute from my slumbers, I should only furnish a conducting signal to a foe equally if not more deadly—I concluded to take my rest in the cabin. The door raised to its former position so as to close entirely the opening, fastening it in its place by the wythes of grape-vine, which I found in long coils conveniently within the cabin. This done, I looked at my inner accommodations. The moon, shining down through one half of the dismantled roof, enabled me to see and to dispose of the massed pine trash, which had once furnished the thatch above. Of this, I made a very comfortable couch in the covered part of my den, which was still in shadow; and, having put my pistols within convenient grasp of my hand, I yielded my farther cares of the night, to the gracious providence, which had hitherto had me in its keeping, a brief prayer for protection, and a few sad thoughts to the memory of poor Helen, and I was soon lost to the farther troubles of consciousness.

I slept very soundly and satisfactorily. My previous excitements and fatigues had given to my slumbers a rare and delightful relish, to confirm the sweetness and efficacy of which, my dreams were of the most soothing and grateful tendency. The past experience of pang was forgotten in their ministerings. Poor Helen was once more a living and loving spirit in my arms. Once more I found myself roving over the wild recesses of Conelachita in her company—my arm about her waist, and both of us as happy, and as little moved by care, as if there had been no other human beings in the world around us. From this happy state, I was suddenly awakened,—I know not how! The moon was shining directly down upon my face. I looked round as if seeking Helen,—becoming aware very slowly of the solemn truth of my loneliness. But I soon became aware of other facts in my condition. The door which I had so carefully put up, as a defence during my slumbers, was removed, and now partly rested against the passage. I could see one of its angles protruding through the space. In the opening, and upon the sill, crouched a form, which, at my first consciousness, seemed to me to be that of a wild animal. I fancied it a bear. Under the momentary impulse, I stretched out my hands to the spot just by my head where I had placed my pistols. They were gone!—and the half scornful chuckle of the intruder, as he beheld my movement, at once informed me by what agency. I started up into a sitting posture and confronted the stranger.

"Be quiet," said he, and I then recognized the voice of Mowbray. "Be quiet—keep your temper and your breath, and all may go well with you."

"Where is Bud Halsey?" I demanded, under I know not what impulse.

"Fortunately for you, not within hearing distance. You are lucky in one thing, that he sent me on this route, instead of taking it himself. But for this your sleep had not been so gently broken!"

"But how did you find me out?"

"Ha! ha! ha! You are a rare person at hide-and-seek. You remind me of that sagacious bird—the ostrich I think it is—that, when pursued by the hunter, buries its head in a hollow, leaving the rest of its carcass to take care of itself. He's a bad scout who thinks, because he can no longer see his enemy, that he himself must needs remain unseen. Why did you hide in the hovel at all—why not in the woods?"

"I was afraid of wolves, and did not dare to light a fire."

"But why not take a tree?"

"I never thought of that! I was, indeed, too much tired, and too sleepy to think at all!"

"Well, that is frank enough,—but, when you determined to take the cabin, you should not have raised the door. That was enough to tell me that somebody was within,—and then you slept in the moonlight! I saw your features distinctly—saw where your pistols lay, and found no difficulty in cutting through grape-vines, letting the door down quietly, and removing your pistols."

This simple statement showed how obtusely I had gone to work, in the stupor caused by fatigue and drowsiness, in rendering myself secure.

"I guarded only against wild beasts—I thought you were far ahead!"—I muttered, as if to excuse my stupidity.

"You thought we were far ahead? Why, what did you know about it?" said Mowbray with some surprise. I hesitated before replying.

"Why should I answer you? Do I not know you to be my enemy? What need of parley between us?"

I spoke this very fiercely. I was now desperate. His coolness,—as I conjectured, what was the feeling of confidence in my capture which filled his mind,—incensed me, and I felt the momentary impulse to spring upon him where he stood.

"Be not wrothy!" he said—"keep cool! You forget, my good fellow, that you are defenceless!"

"Are you sure of that?" I demanded.

He held up my own pistols as I spoke.

"What are these?"

"True,—but I have this!"—and I drew the dirk from my bosom with which Bush Halsey had provided me.

He cocked both of the pistols as I answered.

"And of what avail would your dirk be, Henry Meadows, against these? I have but to draw the trigger of either. I know the pistols and you know my aim. But a truce to this,—you do not yet know me. I do not seek your life. I will save it if you will suffer me. As I said before, it is fortunate that Bush Halsey sent me on this route instead of taking it himself."

I interrupted him.

"Speak to me as an honest man—as *a man*, Mowbray. Do I understand you? Can I believe you? Do you not mean to betray me once more, as you did when you devised the scheme for robbing the supposed agent?"

"How know you that?" he demanded.

In brief, I told him of the position I had kept when Bud Halsey, Warner, and himself stopped for dinner at the spring. How, hanging over their heads, I had heard all their conversation.

"You heard, then, the insolence of this bearded tyrant? You saw what I had to endure—I, a gentleman born and bred, at the hands of the ruffian. You heard,—you say? you heard!"

"Every syllable."

"And you cannot understand why I would thwart the scoundrel—why I would save you?—nay, why I should show you how to put a bullet through his brains? All this will I do! Are you ready to second me? Will you play a desperate game for your life?"

"Try me! If you speak me fairly, the thing may be done. They are but two, and we are—"

"Wronged—and of equal number. Be it so! To prove to you that I am in earnest, here are your pistols. Sound them—see that they are charged. Take nothing on trust. All right?"

"Yes!"

"Now hear me! You chose for your place of rest, the very region where we proposed to lie in wait for you. 'Raccoon Crossings' has three tracks, each leading to an old Indian encampment. You happened to choose the one least likely to have been chosen by one seeking concealment. It lies almost with sight of the road, and was probably the only track you happened to see. It was for this reason that Bud Halsey sent me on this route. He took for granted that you would be more likely to be encountered on either of the others. To one of these he sent Warner, the other he pursued himself. The third, and least likely, under ordinary calculations, to have brought you up, he assigned to me, for no better reason that I can conjecture, but that he suspects me. He suspects me of being privy to your flight, and some singular circumstances, which I need not tell you now, contributed to make his suspicions natural and strong. It will probably increase your confidence in my present plan, when I tell you that, being under his suspicion, I am probably marked out as his next victim, and he only brought me with him, from the Swamp, that I might be under his own eye till the proper moment of dealing with me. A common cause unites us. Are you ready?"

"For what?"

"For what?—Why, blood!—Death!—what else? Do you fear? Will you not fight?"

"Fear! no! Be not so violent! I like harsh language as little as yourself. All I wish to know is what you design—your plan. I have no notion of striking like a blind man in the dark."

"Very good! I understand you. I am a little irritable—half mad, indeed! I feel that I am just sane enough to do mischief, as I certainly am to design it. Here, then, you wait. Keep your den—keep in the dark corner,—while I go and bring Halsey."

"Would it not be better to go him?"

"No! no! It is better as I tell you. I will bring him here. You will keep still—keep dark. I will lead the way into your den, and when he comes, be sure and make your mark upon him. I will be ready to follow up the blow. Only be sure to the right man. I am not quite prepared to be laid by the heels—far from it—far from it—yet I have an ugly notion that my time is not far off. Be you sure of your man, that's all. Look to your pistols—have them cocked, and in readiness,—and, above all things, be cool—be firm—do nothing in a hurry!"

Having thus counselled me, he warned me where to dispose myself, and proceeded to replace my door, which he made me fasten on the inside precisely as I had fastened it before.

"He will probably insist upon the removal of the door himself, for he fancies nobody can do such things half so skillfully. Should this be the case, he may, and probably will, enter the cabin first. In this event, you will act without waiting for me, only taking care that I am not immediately behind him. You will easily know him by his superior bulk. You cannot well confound us, unless you are alarmed beyond measure, which I hardly think will be the case. Be of good heart—you will need all of its strength in half an hour."—With these words, he disappeared.

CHAPTER TWENTY-SIX

As all the particulars in my situation were known to himself, I was content that he should have the management of the affair. It is true, some doubts of his good faith occasionally disturbed me, but they were soon dissipated with the reflection that, had he meant me mischief, nothing would have been more easy than to have carried out his purpose while I slept. He had disarmed me of my most effective weapons,—had afterwards restored them to me,—and, besides, the manner of the man amply denoted the sincerity of those denunciations of his principal, in which he so violently dealt. Still, though resolved to confide in him, I felt very reluctant to await the outlaw in the close den in which I was cabined. Could I have been sure of his route in approaching, I should have certainly gone forth and waylaid him. But the more I reflected, the more I felt the prudence of leaving the matter to Mowbray. At all events, I *was* weaponed! I could do mischief! I could make my enemy pay dearly for his conquest, if he succeeded in obtaining it. I was resolved, *not alone*, to perish,—and, above all things, not to suffer myself to be taken alive! I had too vivid a recollection of that humiliating half-death, by the rope, which I had already undergone at the hands of this butcher.

A more tedious hour than that which followed, I never passed in all my life. My head, meanwhile, was filled with a thousand doubts, suspicions and apprehensions—but, as the more manly course, after all, is to give no half confidence to your ally, I yielded myself up to patience with all my philosophy. To keep quiet, in the one position, in the guise of sleep, was the most difficult of all efforts, and required the utmost inflexibility of nerve. This was the last and most urgent necessity, since I was not to know at what moment the enemy would peer into my premises. A thousand times I fancied whispers and approaches from without. The lifting of a dried leaf

by the wind,—the straining or the sighing of a bough under the same
pressure—these would make my heart beat and jump with the liveliest
anxiety. But I may say, confidently, that I succceeded in quelling my impatience, so as to maintain a position of the utmost physical inflexibility.
I do not think, after the first three minutes succeeding the departure of
Mowbray, that I stirred a muscle. I very well know that I did not move a
limb. Those three minutes I devoted to stirring the priming in my pistols
and putting them on cock—shrouding myself as closely as possible in the
darkest corner of my den, and putting myself just in that position which
would enable me to command the entrance, with the best possible
prospect of doing my work efficiently.

Thus prepared, I endured the hour—for it was fully that—of interval,
which followed the departure of Mowbray, before I became conscious of
his return. The ears of him who watches for his foe are singularly keen and
apprehensive. Miss Baillie, in one of her plays, has a happy illustration of
this exquisite nicety of sense, under such circumstances. I cannot say that
I heard the approach of Bud Halsey, at the very moment when I yet *knew*
that he was nigh. The instinct of hate or love, is a nicer sense than any
which we have in ordinary. It *is* an instinct—a sort of spiritual sense,
which, leaping the ordinary outworks of nature, takes in the coming events
long before they have cast a shadow over the citadel. I knew that my enemy
was nigh, though I did not hear a footstep—not a whisper reached my
ears—not a sound disturbed the familiar silence,—yet I felt that he was
breathing in the same atmosphere with myself. I felt my heart bound—I
felt my pulses quicken—but I was prepared for the worst! Fully ten
minutes followed of the most nervous anxiety. Still, not a sound—not a
movement! Cautious, indeed, were the approaches of the outlaw, and
though, every moment, more and more impatient for action, yet the very
caution of mine enemy tended to the increase of my strength. At length I
was made conscious of a sound, and, an instant after, the light of the moon
glinted from the blade of a knife, which I now perceived to be working
upon the wythes which fastened the door. A few moments sufficed to sever
them on each side, and I then saw that the door, which was a massive one,
was gently, and with ease, lifted from without, and lodged on the inside,
resting against one of the posts. The figure of the person by whom this was
done, was now partially apparent to me, but, as the front of the house was
in shadow, I could not sufficiently distinguish the individual. Could I have
been sure of my man, nothing would have been more easy than to have

shot him where he stood. But I suffered him to enter, which he did, so cautiously, that, though I saw him approach, I never heard a footfall. One more step brought him into the light of the moon, and then, thrusting one of my pistols forward, I pulled trigger upon him. To my utter consternation the weapon gave no report. The flint gave no fire. Before I could present the second pistol, I heard an exclamation from the lips of Mowbray, at the entrance—a single "Ha!" in tones of mortification, and I then beheld him dart upon the outlaw, while he was advancing upon me, and strike him twice in the back. A terrible yell burst from the lips of Bud Halsey, as he turned upon his assailant.

"Traitor!" he exclaimed, "it is you!"

As he turned, with this exclamation, I sprang forward, clapped my remaining pistol to his head and fired—this time with effect. My bullet went through his brain at the very moment when, grasping Mowbray by the throat with one hand, with the other he drove the bowie knife, which had been destined for my bosom, through that of my confederate. Halsey sunk down lifeless, in a heap at my feet; while Mowbray, with outstretched arms, staggered backward, and leaned for a moment against the unhung door, which shook beneath his frame. He spoke but a few words, but they belonged not to the present scene or circumstances.

"Raise my voice, my brethren—cry aloud,—the time is at hand."

"Mowbray!" said I, grasping his body and endeavoring to support him, as I saw that he was about to fall.

"Ah!" said he, with momentary consciousness, "I see how it is! There's no use now! But tell her—tell her all." His lips parted in hurried and frequent murmurs. I let him down gently upon the pine straw.

"Tell her what?—tell *who?*—name her, that I may know."

"What!" he exclaimed, with a momentary recovery of strength, "have you not heard?—have you not understood me?"

"Not a word—not a syllable!"

"Great God!—then it's too late!" and the tears gushed from his eyes. Still he muttered, seemed anxious to make me hear, grasped my arm, and, with a final effort to lift himself, sunk away, and expired in a faint shriek, the appalling sound of which I sometimes hear in my dreams, even to this hour.

CHAPTER TWENTY-SEVEN

I need not say, that for the moment, I was completely stunned by the rapid occurrence of these events, so equally terrible and unexpected. There was my enemy at my foot insensible—my powerful enemy, slain, and without striking a stroke in his defence, by my inexperienced hand—the hand which he either did or affected to despise. True, I had my justification, for I slew him while he was hot in pursuit of my own life. There, too, beside him, lay my confederate,—the unhappy Mowbray, whose own wild and ungovernable passions had defrauded of all the high human hopes, which good family, good education, and rare intellectual endowments, might, under better auspices of morality, have ensured to his endeavors. The first feeling of stupor over, and I sat looking upon his stiffening frame, and vague staring eyes, glistening ghastly in the moonlight, with thick-coming fancies. I remembered his presentiment of evil but a little hour before— the bewildered and only half coherent hope which he expressed for life in the same moment—I remembered his temporary alliance with me—to me it mattered not the motive—by which my life had been saved—and I felt the tears, hot and large, come crowding into my eyes. What would I not have given, could I have heard those last words which he could not artic- ulate, and which seemed to be charged with such weighty interest to his feelings, in the last struggles of his living consciousness! Could he have lived only for repentance! Could I have only been able to convey to the bereaved and mourning wife, the wo-stricken mother, the relatives and friends, the assurance that he died in prayer, and not without a hope! But all was a blank in that last terrible moment, over which let the mortal curtain fall forever.

I was roused from my musings by the necessity for self-preservation. There was still an enemy upon my track. With the thought, I drew myself out of the moonlight. I stole forth in the shadows of the house, and from tree to tree around it, listening for the footfalls of danger. I heard none but my own. Still, there was danger, and it behooved me to prepare for it. I hurried back to the hovel—re-possessed myself of the pistol which had failed me, and which I had cast to the ground when it became necessary to use the other—picked the edges of the flint with the handle of my dagger,—and thus, partially sure of this weapon, I proceeded to make a hurried examination of the dead bodies, in order to possess myself of theirs. I found an armory. Bud Halsey carried three pistols himself, and a bowie knife; while, from the belt of Mowbray, I plucked two more. I secured them all, not so much with the thought that I should need them, but simply to prevent other hands from using them against me. Thus armed, I stole from the hovel, and made my way in the direction of the main *trace* from which I had departed.

I had two objects before me—to find a horse, and to elude or frighten Warner. In all probability, I should be compelled to effect the latter, in order to secure the former object. Where the horses were haltered, was to be ascertained. Probably, they were in this man's keeping. He and they were to be searched for, and at some hazard. But I gave myself up confidingly to the gracious providence that had carried me so far through, and went forward with a free but cautious footstep. If he had heard the shot, which—within three miles, in the deep recesses of night, he was likely to have done,—in all probability he would make his way towards the spot whence it issued. I might then look to meet him. At all events, I was to seek out the other two pathways or 'Crossings,'—whether I looked for him or the horses. In the midst of my doubts and musings, I heard the faint hootings of an owl. It was barely possible that this was a signal. Certainly, owls enough, of the feathered tribe, might be expected in such a region. But I knew how much the outlaws were in the habit of relying upon their powers of imitation, in communicating to one another, under circumstances of danger or difficulty. One thing struck me as suspicious. I did not hear the almost immediate answer to this summons, with which the mate of the owl usually acknowledges the signal. I paused a sufficient time to admit of this, and then determined to remain where I was, under the close cover of a tree, at least for a little space of time. Five minutes had not elapsed, when a second hooting, now more distinct, was echoed through the forest. I determined to try my powers of imitation also, and I sent forth a most vigorous, if not equally dulcet response of "Hoo!—Hoo!—Hoo! hoo! hoo!" There came a ready answer! With the answer I retreated, once more, towards the place of conflict—pausing, after I had gone a certain distance, and waiting for a farther signal. I did not wait for it long, and I was delighted to find that the fellow seemed following the sound. I gave it him again from where I stood, then retreated another space, and waited his approach. Again the cry, and again the answer. I now discovered that he was fairly in the *'crossing'* which led to my den. Here then, I took my stand, within five steps of the path upon which he came, with my person fully concealed in the thicket, yet with the muzzle of my pistols commanding the track and every thing that might come upon it. And now the question occurred to me, shall I—can I—shoot the fellow down from my ambush, or shall I suffer him to go forward, then, hurrying down the road which he had left, leave him to find the bodies, while I sought for the horses. But I had little time for determining my course. There was no choice. The fellow came on horseback! Even while I meditated the question, his horse thundered down the avenue. I resolved on the most merciful expedient, and as the steed appeared in sight, I gave him my bullet. The beast dashed aside against a huge tree, then fell forwards, with a tremendous concussion, to the ground. I had no time to lose. I rushed forward, and as I broke through the bushes, Warner cried out to me:—

"Captain,—Mr. Mowbray—it's me,—Warner—what have you done? Help me! I'm half crushed under the horse. I reckon he's done for. He don't move!"

"Villain!" I cried, bestraddling him, as he lay with one leg and thigh completely under the animal. "Villain!—this moment is your last!"

"How! Who's this?" he screamed—making, at the same time, a vain effort at resistance;—one of his hands striving hard to find its way into his bosom, against which my knee was strenuously pressed.

"Do not move—do not struggle—I have no wish to kill you,—but unless you are quiet I will do so."

"Is it you, Mr. Meadows?"

"Ay! you came too late."

"Who fired before?"

"I did."

"At whom?"

"Your master—Bud Halsey—and he lies as stiff and silent as your horse."

"Grim!—you don't say so."

"It is true as gospel."

"And Mr. Mowbray?"

"He was killed by Bud Halsey."

"I looked for that!" said the fellow, very coolly. "Well, Squire, if it's true what you say, I reckon I must give in! But help me out of this fix, for mercy's sake—I'm afeard the leg's smashed."

"Not till I've emptied your bosom of what it's got in it, my good fellow. Let us see."

He offered no objections to my search, and I drew from his bosom and waist, with some difficulty, a pair of pistols, a bowie knife, and an ordinary *couteau de chasse*,—for Warner was a "master of the pleasant sports of Venerie." Though I searched narrowly, I found nothing more, likely to endanger my safety,—and, these secured, I proceeded to give him all the help I could in extricating him from the body of the horse. This was no easy task, for the animal was one of considerable size, and the roots and vines where he had fallen offered many obstructions. Besides, it appeared, from the way in which he lay, that Warner could do little for himself. When at length relieved, he did not rise. He strove, but could not. A moment's examination sufficed to show that his right leg was shattered.

"What am I to do?" was the mournful exclamation of the ruffian.

"I'll tell you," was my answer. "Where have you left the horses of Bud Halsey and Mowbray?"

He gave me directions where I should find them, and leaving him where he lay, I at once went after them. They were soon found, and choosing the best, which was a noble black of Bud Halsey, I mounted him, and led the other to Warner.

"Now," said I, "there is but one way for you. I will help you to mount the horse of Mowbray, which is a short animal, and as you are a good rider, you can keep on with me to the first settlement, where you can get surgical assistance, or at all events, the best assistance that the neighborhood affords. What say you to that?"

"Thank you, sir,—but I know a better way. Only help me to get on the horse, sir, and then, with your leave, we'll part company. It's not every day that I can visit the settlements, and it may be as much as my neck's worth to go in your company."

"Do you think I would betray you?" I said, with loathing.

"No! sir, oh! no! I reckon I know you better,—but you'd find it difficult to answer for me, seeing as how I'd find it impossible to answer for myself; and then, again, there's no need for me to go that way for help, when I can get quite as good or better in the Swamp."

"Can you? Are you sure that you can reach the Swamp?"

"Oh! very sure; for that matter I shall find help long before I get there."

"Be it so," I answered. "You know best.—You have your choice. You are your own master." He signified his readiness to make the effort, and fastening the horse of Mowbray to a sapling close beside him, I threw my whole strength into the effort, and raised him erect—he resting, for an instant, upon his sound leg, while I lifted him to my shoulder, and finally to the saddle, in the stirrup of which, planting the foot of his unbroken limb, he contrived, with my assistance, to fling the shattered member across. The effort was one of great suffering, and at one moment I thought the fellow would have fainted. But he was a tough villain, and had been in such scrapes before.

"It's not the first time," said he, with a groan; "I've had the same leg smashed before, and I reckon it wont be the last."

"Take care," said I, "the next time, it isn't your neck!"

"Ah! Squire," said the scoundrel, with a chuckle, "it's not *my* neck only that's in danger!"

The reminiscence might have been fatal to him an hour before; but I suffered the insolence to pass unpunished. Certainly, the fellow deserved to go scot-free who could be content to joke under such circumstances. I saw him fairly started, in very tolerable strength and spirits, and became satisfied that he should thus depart, from the coolness and confidence which he manifested.—He uttered his thanks and acknowledgments very civilly, and, seeing him fairly under way, I also took the saddle. In a few moments he was off in a smart canter, while, taking the opposite direction, I proceeded also at a similar pace. Whether he lived or died, recovered his limb, or went lame through life, I cannot say. He has no farther interest in my story. For this, almost as brief a paragraph will suffice. I reached Leaside without further adventure or interruption of any moment. I stopped a night with 'plain Yannaker,' who eyed my black with the wistful eyes of one who had his doubts and curiosities. But he asked no questions. Some day, Yannaker shall make a story of his own.—How my mother blessed me and kissed me, and welcomed me home—how she looked into my face and wondered at its sedateness—how my father pressed me for a narration, which, until this moment I have shared with none,—these call for no farther development. But there was a cloud upon my brow which neither had ever beheld there before—and there was an abstraction in my glance, which was strangely at variance with the imperious and direct gaze with which, before that season, I had met every other eye. In the brief space of two months, I had counted years by moments. I had crowded the events of a long life, into the limits of a single moon.

CONCLUSION

Seven years after these events, there was a general clearing out of the out-laws, from the swamp retreats of Conelachita. The circumstances distin-guishing the movement of that popular phrenzy, by which this great result was effected, have already been chronicled in history and illustrated by romance. Under less circumspect leaders, the outlaws had lost much of their prudence and adroitness; and, indeed, the condition of the country had become less favorable to their operations. Population of a more permanent and industrious, and, consequently, more honest description, had been steadily pouring in, and the ultimate extinction of the Indian title to the lands, was an event, of itself, to strike a fatal blow at the security of the 'government-against-law' in Conelachita. How the people, furious in the consequence of the most frequent and audacious murders, to say nothing of robberies, rushed *en masse* into the swamp-fastnesses, and, with shot, and sabre-stroke, and halter, put an end to the dynasty of the outlaw, in that quarter, needs only to be glimpsed here. The affair was one of immense interest to the country at large, and of a peculiarly delicate interest to me. I read the accounts of the progress of the *regulators*, as they appeared from time to time in the papers of the Southwest, with an exciting and painful anxiety. The fate of the poor father—of the really good Bush Halsey—unfortunately cursed with so bad a brother—was, in particular, a matter upon which I brooded with an almost unremitting thought. I could not forget how dear he was to me, not only as the father of my wife, but on his own account. From him I had met with nothing but what was considerate in kindness, and affectionate in consideration. I resolved finally, in order to quiet my own thoughts, to seek out his fate—to see whether he had perished with the rest—in the indiscriminate massacre which had befallen the miserable wretches, with whom he was, but *of* whom he was not! Circumstances were now not so unfavorable to such a search. The country along the route was tolerably settled. The rogues had generally given way to a better race of men. Even 'Plain Yannaker' had made tracks, and removed with his teraphim into the wilderness. Travelling was secure. Broad roads were opened through regions once traversed only by the Indian foot-trail; and, with bitter-sweet recollections rising at every step, I once more penetrated the well-known and once mysterious recesses of Conelachita. How, as I went along, the present dilated in homily upon the past. I flattered myself that I had grown wiser, and this notion reconciled me to many a gloomy recollection. But in these I will not indulge.

Once more I found the cottage in the Swamp, in which I had wedded my poor Helen. It was in the possession of a squatter, whom I bought out, taking care that my titles in the land-office should supply any deficiencies in his. But, ere I made my way down the stream upon which I had sped that fatal night with Helen and her father, I recognized, with a thrill of the keenest emotion, the little bayou, in the scoop of which our bark had lain, hidden by the overhanging shrubs and willows, in waiting for Bush Halsey. It was there that she had rested in my arms—silent, tearful, with the love within her heart,—and O! how little dreaming of the sudden and terrible fate which stood in waiting for her, but a little mile below. I turned from the spot with heart too tremulous to be trusted to contemplation. Then, as the fatal point rose in view, on which, crouching with his myrmidons, Bud Halsey issued the stern order, and sped the murderous shot, I shuddered with horrors such as did not thrill me then. Little then did I foresee the brutal haste, the reckless resolution, with which that fierce uncle would carry out his threat. I groaned from the bottom of my heart,—and the paddle escaped my grasp. This incident awakened me, and I recovered myself. It was not a long while before we reached the island. There, we drew the boat ashore, and I hurried, without delay, toward the secluded spot where the woman of my heart lay buried. I was met by a bowed form—a diminutive, withered, white-headed old man—almost bent double. His hair, of the most silvery whiteness, covered his back. His beard was similarly white and long. It was he! It was the father! He knew me at a glance; and, as if I could have but a single object, he took me by the hand gently, and said:—

"Come"—in the sweetest accents, and led me at once to the grave of Helen!

THE END.

AFTERWORD

Eighteen forty-five was a banner year for Simms: though in it he published nothing worthy in his most celebrated literary form—the large two-volume novel—he never again matched the diversity, variety, and overall excellence of his feat of bringing out in a single year exceptional work in three distinct genres: *The Wigwam and the Cabin*, two volumes of short stories; *Views and Reviews in American Literature, History and Fiction*, two volumes of essays; and *Helen Halsey: or, The Swamp State of Conelachita*, a short novel or novelette—a total of five volumes with literary merit of high order. Almost without debate *The Wigwam and the Cabin* has been acclaimed Simms's best collection of short stories, and *Views and Reviews* his best collection of literary and political essays. Although critical recognition of *Helen Halsey* has been slight, partly because the book experienced but a single small paperback printing (selling for twenty-five cents) and has long been unavailable, Simms himself, confident of its worth as "one of [his] most successful performances," constantly sought its republication in an authentic hardback edition[1]—and would rejoice to know of its inclusion in the Arkansas Edition. Written at a time when his literary prowess was at or near its zenith, *Helen Halsey* is (as Simms put it) "particularly good" in style and "rapid and truthful" in narration (*L*, I, 420). *Helen Halsey* substantiates the view that Simms excelled in the writing of the short novel or novelette—what he called "regularly planned . . . novels in little" (*L*, III, 342).

Though the shortest of Simms's Border novels, *Helen Halsey* nevertheless *is* a Border novel: in Simms's mind it was clearly a member of the series of frontier novels originating with *Guy Rivers*, *Richard Hurdis*, and *Border Beagles*. Except in brevity it hardly fits the category of Simms's short novels, a diverse classification that includes *Martin Faber* and *Paddy McGann*—each with little in common with the other and even less with *Helen Halsey*. Subtitled "A Tale of the Borders," *Helen Halsey* shares much with the first three Border novels: a frontier setting, strong sense of place, and graphic description of wilderness; depiction of corruption of civil, legal, and religious officials; thematic interest in widespread organized crime, the propensity for violence, and the prevalence of vigilantism; and recognition of sociological and psychological bases for crime.

In explaining the nature of his work to Rufus W. Griswold in 1845, Simms himself made a significant point:

> Belonging to the same family with Guy Rivers, are Richard Hurdis,
> Border Beagles, Beauchampe, Helen Halsey,—some ten or a dozen
> volumes,—distinguished by great activity of plot, vehement &
> passionate personality, and pictures & sketches of border character &
> border scenery, in which I claim to be equally true and natural. There
> are running through all these works, a strong penchant to moral and
> mental analysis. (*L*, II, 225)

As has been pointed out in the Introduction, *Helen Halsey* adds the
element of marital conflict to the congenital violence of the frontier, and
in this respect bears a strong resemblance to the two Border novels
immediately preceding it, *Confession; or, The Blind Heart. A Domestic
Story* (1841) and *Beauchampe, or The Kentucky Tragedy, A Tale of Passion*
(1842).

Simms apparently found the basic idea for *Helen Halsey* in a story
entitled "The Outlaw's Daughter," which appeared in the Charleston journal *Cosmopolitan: An Occasional* in 1833 when Simms was its coeditor—
or, perhaps, to be more nearly accurate, its coauthor.[2] "The Outlaw's
Daughter," written by one of the journal's coauthors, Edward Carroll, a
longtime friend of Simms, contains the situational framework that Simms
loosely adopted in writing *Helen Halsey:* the concept of a proud, sensitive
girl whose loving relationship with her outlaw father subsequently leads to
her violent death. Using only the bare, broad outline of "The Outlaw's
Daughter" in molding his own narrative, Simms shifts the time from just
before the Revolutionary War to the early nineteenth century, the setting
from South Carolina to "some of the wildest regions of the South-West"
(1),[3] and the point of view from omniscient narrator to limited first
person. He also substantially alters as well as expands the plot: he drops the
brother-sister relationship of "The Outlaw's Daughter" and substitutes a
tempestuous love affair that evolves into a husband-wife relationship; and
he changes the outlaw father (loving to be sure, in both stories) from a
strong, willful adventurer attracted to violence into an indecisive weakling
trapped in a life of crime from which he has no will to escape. And in
changing the locale of the action from South Carolina to an unspecified
Gulf coast state like Louisiana or Mississippi, Simms, it is important to
remember, retains the swamp setting essential to the plot. There are other
bits of evidence that Simms had Carroll's story in mind. The heroine of
"The Outlaw's Daughter" is named Ellen (Rogers): Simms originally
thought of his own outlaw's daughter as Ellen (Halsey)—indeed, in the
first mention by Simms of *Helen Halsey,* its title is "Ellen Halsey, or My Wife

against my Will," and demonstrating that the title is not in error, he adds the telling comment: "Ellen Halsey will of itself make over 100 pages" (letter to James Lawson, June 12, 1843; *L*, I, 354). It is noteworthy, too, that in the text of *Helen Halsey* itself Simms once inadvertently calls his heroine "Ellen" (69).

The crux of all this is not that *Simms* borrowed from Carroll—there is no recorded acknowledgment on Simms's part—but rather that an author perceived from reading or observation the germ for a story, planted it in his memory, and later nurtured its germination and flowering: the process, described by Henry James, by which a writer's mind turns a rough idea, borrowed from reading or observation, into something of his own, whose source is recognizable but whose final artistic form is original. With *Helen Halsey* Simms has used "The Outlaw's Daughter" for his starting point; he has followed his own imagination and his own purposes in transforming a conceptual sketch into a novel (short though it be) that adeptly fits what he had already begun—a series of fictional portrayals of the American frontier as it pushes ever westward.

In *Helen Halsey,* as in each of the Border novels, Simms establishes a realistic sense of place by vividly describing the wildlife and the landscape of the lush swampland wilderness:

> The trees began to cast a longer, denser shadow across my path, and the sun glimmered faintly, sprinkling the open space with a cluster of beaded gold-drops.... Once, a couple of deer glided over the road from one thicket to another ... and, as the sun disappeared, a couple of screech owls commenced a most gloomy death-duett.... The moon rose.... She poured a steady blaze of light across the path. [111]

Simms's writing also accurately reflects the manners and customs of the frontiersmen, as revealed in the early conversation between the landlord of a border public house, Jeph Yannaker, and the traveling narrator (later identified as Henry Meadows) who addresses Yannaker as "Mister":

> "Don't mister me, stranger,—I'm plain Jeph Yannaker to travellers, and Yannaker to them that knows me. I'm agin making a handle for a man's name before you can trust yourself to take hold of it."
>
> "No offence, Jeph Yannaker—I only speak as I've been accustomed."
>
> "No offence, to be sure,—it's your teaching, stranger, but here in our parts, where people's scarce, and the sight of one's neighbor does the heart good, a handle to his name seems to push him too far out of the reach of a friendly gripe. It's a stiff, cold sort of business, this mistering and squiring—will do well enough among mere gentlemen,

and lawyers, and judges, and such sort of cattle,—but out here, where a look upon the hills and swamps seems to give a man a sort of freedom, it's a God's blessing that we have few such people here. Here we're nothing but men, just as God made us,—not to speak of a little addition, in the shape of jacket and breeches, made out of blue or yellow homespun." [12]

Meadows is intrigued to witness a country dance, announced by "the discordant twang of a half-tuned fiddle," which attracts more than thirty persons of both sexes who come from "a space of country twenty miles around" to crowd into Yannaker's ramshackle hall. The dance participants are depicted in colorful detail:

> The men were stout fellows all, of the true farm-yard breed, famous at the flail, and with fists, whose seeming efficiency reminded me more than once of the powers ascribed to those of Maximin, the Gaul, who could fell a bullock at a blow.... Their costume was that of the farm-yard. Plain blue or yellow homespun, rough shoes, and, though the winter had fairly set in, many were the bronzed and naked breasts displayed by the open shirt of coarse cotton.

Similarly unencumbered was their attitude toward the dance: "The frolic, so far as they were concerned, was evidently *extempore*. They had been suffered no time for the toilet. But this did not seem greatly to abash them. They... dashed forward, each to his favorite lass, as coolly and confidently as if fashion had received her dues." Their behavior evokes in Meadows a positive assessment: "And there was, in this very freedom, a sort of savage grace, which greatly tended to lessen the rudeness of its general aspects" (4).

The women at the dance were more self-conscious and contrived in their dress than the men, leading Meadows to reflect that they "lacked the graces—however inferior—which distinguished the deportment of the men." He elaborates: "They sat, stiffly and awkwardly, like so many waxen figures, each on her stool, as if troubled with a disgusting apprehension that any unwise movement would overturn the fair fabric of her present state, and be equally fatal to head-dress, handkerchief and happiness." He notes, however, "one exception to this uniform display of ostentation and awkwardness" (5)—that one exception being, of course, Helen Halsey herself, whose beauty and poise leave the narrator spellbound.

Though Simms paints an attractive picture of the openness, the color, the freedom from formality of the frontier setting, his chief focus is to give an unflinching picture of its other side—its wildness, its violence, its terror,

its corruption. One aspect of backwoods life that Simms focuses on in
Helen Halsey is its violence toward women—particularly those unfortunate habitués of the Southwest border who suffer kinds of indignities
and abuse unthinkable in polite society. Witness, for instance, Meadows's
detailed but almost lackadaisical account of a kind of brutality so common in everyday frontier experience that it was, in effect, condoned—
regrettable perhaps, but inevitable; at least it was considered too trivial for
real concern:

> That day I rode forty miles, and slept at the wigwam of a mulatto, who
> gave his wife,—an Indian woman—a sound drubbing in my very sight,
> and in spite of all my expostulations. & I believe the only offence on
> her part was that she had suffered the fish to burn, which his imperial
> highness had caught for his own, and which furnished a very sorry
> portion of my supper. She probably deserved all that she got—was a
> sulky hag, of fierce, black, revengeful aspect, who, in all probability will
> have a day of recknoing [reckoning] with him on this very account. My
> interposition saved her from a part of the flogging—at all events, such
> was his assurance to me while it was in progress; and with this I had
> to be satisfied. [104]

When put in juxtaposition with what Meadows, the young romantic,
earlier conceptualized about "our Southern women"—his description of
them as "delicate," "languid," and "luxurious," yet "with souls, in some
respect, very far superior . . . to those of the most heroic men" (91)—the
contrast in attitude toward women is stark indeed. Simms was not unaware
of this inequity in society's attitude toward women—the cultivated woman
of charm versus the rough, ill-bred woman of low station—and he quietly
but effectively reveals the injustice of both perception and treatment
through the thoughts and observations of the figure of Henry Meadows,
who though usually compassionate, remains apparently oblivious to this
own lack of sensitivity to the plight of the one and to his exaltation of the
nobility of the other. Simms's portrayal of women, as this instance suggests,
is far more complex and sophisticated than has yet been demonstrated, and
an in-depth study of his characterization of women is an urgent need of
Simms scholarship. His accurate perception of the role of women on the
frontier, as leaders as well as victims, is a salient feature of his Revolutionary
and Border Romances.

Although it is not labeled the Mystic Confederacy or Brotherhood, as
it was in *Richard Hurdis* and *Border Beagles,* a similar brotherhood of
criminals exists in *Helen Halsey.* As Bud Halsey, leader of the gang

garrisoned in the well-protected swamp headquarters at Conelachita, explains to Henry Meadows, masquerading as a fugitive wanted for murder:

> Here you are safe, as long as you choose to remain. You know what we are, and must abide by our laws. . . . This affair [the alleged murder] may blow over—your friends may succeed in hushing it up, and then you may return in safety to your family. Nay, even we may do something towards this result, however strange you may think it. Outlaws ourselves, we have friends not only among those who obey, but those who administer the laws. [28–29]

In fact, in some ways, the organization of Bud Halsey is even more sophisticated than that of Clement Foster *(Richard Hurdis)* or Ellis Saxon *(Border Beagles):* to a degree unmatched by the Mystic Confederacy, Halsey's brotherhood is a community concerned with social amenities for its members, as well as being a well-hidden, military-like fortress for their safety and protection. Not only did Mowbray perform ecclesiastical functions like weddings and funerals, he also preached sermons, held religious services, and provided counseling for stricken members of the clan, men and women. It is also apparent that recreational activities such as picnicking, hiking, boating, fishing, game-playing, and nature study were part of the everyday life of the inhabitants of Conelachita. As Bud Halsey explains to Henry Meadows, "You must not suppose yourself without privileges. Your bounds are not too close for sport and moderate exercise. This island . . . is free to you in every quarter" (36). Though Bud Halsey's syndicate as depicted by Simms is smaller in size and more restricted in space than the Mystic Confederacy, which spread from Virginia to Louisiana, the centralization of functions decreed by the leader seems to have made the gang not only easier to command, but generally efficient in all its operation.

Characterization of the rough and resolute resident of the frontier is a forte of Simms in his Border Romances, and *Helen Halsey* is no exception. The contrasting characters of the Halsey brothers, Bud and Bush, are particularly adeptly drawn, each with a mixture of good and evil, though Bud is preponderantly evil—strong and maliciously aggressive—and Bush is essentially good—well-intentioned and sensitive—yet also self-centered and easily manipulated. It is interesting to see each brother in the eyes of the other; both are presented as intelligent men, not only capable of understanding the inherent temperament of the other but also aware of the sociological basis for a belligerent disposition. For instance, Bush Halsey's estimate of Bud Halsey is terse and accurate, demonstrating a consciousness of the effect of environment in the molding of character: "My brother is a violent man. We differ, as you many see, materially in temper. He has been rendered more violent, and perhaps unjust by frequent injustice." Stating, "[W]e have both suffered from a like cause; but it is my fortune to remain somewhat human," he offers in way of explanation one significant and distinguishing feature: "possibly, because I have been left one human blessing which was denied to him. I am still a father" (36), On the other hand, Bud Halsey's analysis of Bush rings equally valid, though the sarcasm and latent resentment are self-revelatory. Bud says menacingly to Henry Meadows:

> Bush Halsey is, in some respects, as great a simpleton as yourself. If he had a voice in the matter, he would send you home to your mother, perhaps fill your pockets with ginger-bread, pat you on the head, bid you go on your way rejoicing, and shed a flood of benevolent tears at your departure. But I am the master here. I am the outlaw! I do and counsel the robberies, and, if you please, I command and execute the murders. You know enough to make the task of confession on my part a very easy one. You know too much! [49]

Simms offers rare insight into the motivations for crime in a power-hungry, egotistical, and revengeful ruffian; his portrayal of indignation and hostility in Bud Halsey is skillfully handled, demonstrating compassion without condolence in its understanding of cause and effect.

But without doubt it is the complex, almost contradictory nature of Bush Halsey that most interests Simms. The author uses Henry Meadows as his vessel of consciousness to record impressions of the elder Halsey:

> My companion was free of speech, and his conversational resources, I soon found, were equally admirable and ample. He was deeply versed in books—he had seen the world, and was not insensible to its refinements. His eye was evidently one accustomed to seek out and discriminate the forms of beauty in external objects, and he frequently drew the regards of mine to this or that point of view in the surrounding landscape, which was either picturesque or fine. [29]

Bush Halsey, according to the narrator-protagonist, "played the country gentleman to perfection," complete with a servant to come at his summons "at the table and get us refreshments" (31). Courtly, polite, and well-read, he not only treated Meadows "with the most marked attention" (31) but delighted him with his nightly conversations described as "thoughtful, tasteful, philosophical." Bush Halsey was also gifted, with a "most exquisite

skill in music. His flute . . . seemed the voice of some complaining angel"
(37), leading Meadows to conclude, "It seemed to me that, if a heart could
ever speak in music, such would have been the strains poured forth by a
breaking one" (31). Yet with all his accomplishments and refinements,
Bush Halsey, whose "worst crime" was bankruptcy, was like putty in the
hands of his rebellious, wrathful brother, who afforded him safe haven in
the swamp hide-out. The narrator describes him as a "good man, meaning
well, and with an excellent mind . . . yet controlled entirely by the superior
will of his brother—a man of inferior intellect" and generalizes: "once a
slave, such a man always remains a slave." So he notes of Bush Halsey:
"From the moment that he yielded to the suggestions of his brother, and
fled from his creditors to the wilderness, from that moment, he yielded
himself up to a bondage, from which he did not now hope to set himself
free" (81). The final irony in the delineation of the two outlaw brothers is
that the daughter who made the difference to the one was ultimately
destroyed by the other, who had no one to redeem his wasted life. Simms's
imagination sustained him well in creating with Bush and Bud Halsey two
of his most memorable characters, distinctively different partners in crime,
each conceived with realism and vigor.

Another compelling, enigmatic character in *Helen Halsey* is Mowbray,
"a gentleman of the Episcopal persuasion" who like Bush Halsey comes
to life with a baffling, seemingly contradictory mixture of humanizing
virtues and vices: "He was a fine looking young man of florid complexion,
a bright blue eye with a restless roving twinkle, which betrayed an unsettled
and capricious disposition. His temperament and the general expression
of his features, showed the presence of strong, unregulated passions"
(57–58). In recounting the history of Mowbray (an assumed name), Simms
satirically reveals hypocrisy within society and church as well as within the
individual whose family and friends cavalierly decided that he "was to be
a parson," reasoning that "when a fellow is too stupid to be a lawyer or
doctor, you must make him a parson" (68, 69). In Mowbray's own words,

> Nobody seemed to regard the moral requisites of the Churchman, as
> at all necessary. Nothing, at least, was said on this part of the subject.
> It was chosen for me as a handicraft—a trade—by which I was to jump
> into a snug living, and have the farther privilege of choosing, as my
> own peculiar property, one of the richest ewes of my flock. [69]

Entering the clergy without conviction or commitment—not a concern
of the church—Mowbray soon discovered that personal hypocrisy within
institutional hypocrisy was the key to advancement. "It requires but little

skill and management ... to win the reputation of great piety; and still less ability, to secure that of eloquence and talent," Mowbray confessed. "I have frequently amused myself, during my brief career in the pulpit, in preaching nonsense-sermons, that were simply complicate and high-sounding, larded at frequent intervals, with biblical phrases" (69–70). Driven by ambition, and without inhibition or piety, Mowbray quickly rose in his profession, won an elegant wife, and prospered in every way:

> I was surrounded by plenty—beauty was in my arms—fortune at my feet—crowds of admirers followed in my steps—troops of friends gathered at my bidding—my voice could still or rouse the multitude— my name was honored wherever spoken—but *I lived a lie!*—and every moment of breath and being was a pang. I do not say that my moral sense revolted ... No! it was my blood, my passions, which, restrained, in order to the acquisition of an object, threatened momently to revenge themselves for the unnatural and uncongenial bondage into which my will had forced them. [72]

Mowbray's fall from fortune and station began when his wife discovered the hypocrisy of his present and the secret debauchery of his past. Religious in the deepest sense, she was shocked by his treachery, and her adoration of him turned into pity and scorn. Unable to cope with her rejection—and above all, with her good intentions to reform him— Mowbray renounced church, home, wife, and infant son and passed on, a renegade, to New Orleans, where he found "sufficient elasticity" for his moral nature in "various theatres of pleasure and dissipation" (76). Concluding his self-history, Mowbray's confession takes on an anguished tone: "You see that I do exult in this depravation. You see that I relate the story of the past without pleasure! That I suffer! That I feel the folly and the sin of all that miserable boy-career, begun in narrow schemes, and finishing in shocking perversion." Addressing the questions he believes must rise in Meadows's mind—"You ask why I do not change—why I stubbornly lie in sin—why I do not regret, repent, retrieve?"—Mowbray describes the tortured nature of his existence: "What if I tell you of my tears, my prayers, my repentance? I do weep! I do repent! But, what is repentance that does nothing but weep? This is mine! I do nothing! My repentance is without results! I cannot pray—I cannot toil—in any work of good!" Ultimately he reveals the terror in his soul:

> There is a terrible power that denies me—that keeps me back from the very first performances of repentance! I dare not ask what is this power! I only feel that its presence is upon me, baffling my purpose,

and mocking at all my hopes! It never can be withdrawn! I am not
suffered to approach the throne of God—I am doomed, utterly
doomed of heaven! [77]

Not even Hawthorne ever suffered a character—not Dimmesdale, not
Goodman Brown, not Ethan Brand—to be so wracked with spiritual
despair as is Simms's Mowbray in this impassioned outburst. If the outcry
did not cleanse the soul of Mowbray, it did affect the mind and heart of
Meadows: "I need not say how much my respect for this unhappy person
had increased" (78).

Simms's in-depth characterization of Mowbray is so multi-faceted that
even this remarkable eruption does not display the full measure of this
volatile man of ambiguity and contradiction. Having genuinely been
moved by Mowbray's apparent remorse and self-chastisement, Meadows
is much taken back by the "wonderful . . . flexibility of this man." "He had
left me," Meadows reflects, "on the day when I had heard his narrative,
looking more like a maniac than a man. Never could I suppose that the
same person would ever smile again. The next day he met me with a bawdy
jest" (80); and several days later, the narrator reports listening, "for the
tenth time, to one of his most licentious stories" (89).

As Meadows observes,

> I found him always thus capricious;—at one moment gloomy, even
> to ferocity, and sometimes touched with a sort of religious fanaticism.
> . . . The next day he was the courtier—all gravity and smiles, and as
> loose in his morals as the most reckless cavalier of the Court of Charles
> the Second—as courtly as Waller, and as licentious as Rochester,—as
> sentimental sometimes as the one, and again as filthily witty as the
> other. He realized the extremes of character more suddenly, in the same
> person, and frequently on the same day, than any other man I ever met.
> I confess that I was not unfrequently pleased with his society—his
> wit—his eloquence—his sentiment. [80]

But Mowbray's characteristic capriciousness does not mitigate his intense
suffering, nor negate his desire for repentance that is able to "toil" in "work
of good," supplanting the futility of "repentance that does nothing but
weep." And his heroic death, coming at the hands of Bud Halsey as a consequence of the clergyman's efforts to save the life of Henry Meadows,
seems to represent—despite his own doubts and those of Meadows—
evidence of a kind of spiritual redemption. The ambiguity surrounding
the last act of Mowbray's life—whether or not it is an evocation of peni-

tence and forgiveness—is in keeping with the ambivalence of his character. All in all, in its depth and complexity, Simms's delineation of the Reverend Mr. Mowbray is a superb accomplishment: Mowbray takes a place by Dimmesdale among outstanding portraits of divines in nineteenth-century American literature.

Although Henry Meadows does not initially strike the reader of *Helen Halsey* as the novel's central character, his importance as Simms's vessel of consciousness through whose eyes, ears, and thoughts all other characters are revealed and the plot itself unfolds has already been alluded to. In some ways, *Helen Halsey* records Henry Meadows's initiation into manhood: the novel follows a young man who leaves home and parents to journey into the wilderness, partly to satisfy his "natural passion for adventure" (16), partly to seek his own identity. As Simms's protagonist-narrator, his restricted point of view imparts to the novel a sense of modernity: *Helen Halsey*, like *Richard Hurdis* seven years before, anticipates the technique of Henry James well before the advent of literary realism. As a young and inexperienced observer, Meadows represents the unreliable narrator whose views are sometimes wrong; but he learns from his mistakes and grows in perceptiveness and wisdom as the novel progresses. He is humanized by his impulsiveness in falling in love with Helen Halsey and by the reckless-ness of his pursuit of her in the face of her own warnings, but, even more important, by his candor in admitting the decline of his ardency for her after, ironically, Bud Halsey forced them to marry. The love affair (central to the plot of the novel) is kept interesting because of young Henry's confessions of his inconstancy. Recognizing that he now feels imprisoned by the marital relationship he once eagerly sought, he confides to the reader, "I was a husband at eighteen. An outlaw's daughter was my bride. Had I left the home of my father for this? What had I become? What was I to become?" (59). Later Meadows confesses, "I strove to hide from my wife, the discontent of which I was now fully conscious" (62)—an effort at concealment totally unsuccessful with his perceptive bride, who quickly noted the change in him. Meadows's admission of his own impetuousness and self-centeredness—and of his wife's patience and thoughtfulness—is also disarming:

> [Helen] was still so loving, so considerate, so desirous to win me to pleasure, to see me happy—and failing,—so sad,—that, when not thinking absolutely and only of myself, my heart smote me for its cold-ness to her. Coldness shall I call it? No! it was not coldness. I had not then any idea that any woman could be half so dear to me as she was,

even in those moments when I felt least satisfied. . . . She was content to do her best to cheer me, to prove that her love for me had not lessened, and she left to the delicate unpremeditated attentions of a fond heart, and tender solicitude, to heal those hurts, which any attempt to probe might only have rendered worse. [63–64]

Much of the effectiveness in Simms's characterization of Meadows stems from the young man's gradual evolvement from wild-eyed romanticism to stoical realism—from reliance on human intuition to dependence on animal instinct. Meadows seems to be gifted in both senses. It was intuition—not a declaration from Helen Halsey—that first informed him that he "was the master of her heart" (33), but it was "instinct—a sort of spiritual sense" that made him aware that his "enemy [Bud Halsey] was nigh, though [he] did not hear a footstep." This is the same animal sixth sense by which Frank Norris's McTeague knows he is being pursued by his enemy, Marcus Schouler. In one short novel Simms has adroitly blended elements of romanticism, realism, and naturalism—though the latter two movements did not yet have names.

Even before Helen Halsey's sudden death—at the hands of her uncle as she, her father, and her husband attempted a desperate escape from Conelachita—had shocked Meadows into realization of his deep love for her, Simms had bit by bit signaled the growth of his protagonist's sense of responsibility and the decline of his self-aggrandizement. Meadows had come full circle: from the passionate young adventurer who visualized Helen Halsey as "the heroine of romance, to be rescued from the bearded giant" (16); to the disillusioned husband who in the skepticism of his self-interest questioned the integrity of his love (63–64); to the self-reliant pragmatist who, adopting the ruse of a con man, "gamed, and drank, and swore" (85) like a blackguard to conceal his escape purpose from Bud Halsey; to a resolute, reflective man of acquired character[4] certain of his courage, his belief, his identity, and the permanence of his love for the woman he had wooed, won, and lost.

The title character herself, Helen Halsey, is not a central figure in the novel in the sense that she reveals herself to the reader; we see her primarily in the consciousness of the narrator, and she is essential in that she is the figure who serves as the catalyst for the narrator's revelation of self. The plot revolves around Helen Halsey: she is the motivator of action in the first half of the book, and she is the person to whom things happen in the second half—the victim of the tragic action in the concluding chapters. She is the heroine of the novel that bears her name, but she is not the central figure—the protagonist-narrator, Henry Meadows, is the central figure.

In *Helen Halsey*, William Gilmore Simms has written another authentic account of the frontier of the Old Southwest, once again displaying, in the well-informed words of Evert Duyckinck, an unmatched prowess as storyteller:

> As a story-teller, I have never met his equal. He has travelled through all the Southern and South-western States, has been among the "up country" farmers, the turpentine manufacturers, the backwoods hunters, and the Indians, and has laid up an apparently inexhaustible supply of stories and anecdotes.... These anecdotes and stories he tells with the greatest zest, and with the skill of an accomplished actor imitating to perfection the dialect, tones, and action, of the various characters introduced.[5]

In summary, the strengths of the novel are in its effective characterization; in its use of a mode of narration that lends it credibility and gives it a surprising air of modernity; but, most of all, in its graphic depiction of the brutality and violence endemic as responsible persons of nobility and courage clashed with the greedy and corrupt exploiters of the land and its people. Though the names and places are fictitious, Simms has painted another realistic picture of a place and time important in American history.

Frontier justice, in the form of vigilantism, had ended the reign of terror at Conelachita with terror of its own—with "the indiscriminate massacre which had befallen the miserable wretches"—and the "rogues had generally given way to a better race of men" (125, 126). American *a priori* progress had again prevailed.

Notes

1. Though never republished in book form, *Helen Halsey*, under the title "The Island Bride," was republished serially in the *New York Fireside Companion* in seven installments in 1869, the year before Simms's death. See Textual Notes, below.

2. Ostensibly the anonymous work of "Three Bachelors," the *Cosmopolitan* first appeared in Charleston in May 1833. Research has shown that the "Three Bachelors" were Simms, Charles Rivers Carroll, and Edward Carroll, all three of whom have been identified as authors of pieces published in the occasional. See John C. Guilds, "William Gilmore Simms and the *Cosmopolitan*," *Georgia Historical Quarterly* 41 (March 1957): 31–41.

It is interesting that *Helen Halsey*, in turn, has been found to contain the basis for a German work by Friedrich Gerstäcker, who translated *The Wigwam and the Cabin* (and perhaps other titles by Simms) into his native tongue. See J. Wesley Thomas, "William Gilmore Simms' 'Helen Halsey' as the Source for Friedrich Gerstäcker's 'Germelshausen,'" *Monatsheft* 45 (March 1953): 141–44.

3. "South West" for Simms and his contemporaries meant, for the most part, the western portions of Georgia and Tennessee, and the entire states of Alabama, Mississippi, and Louisiana—and, slightly later, Arkansas, Texas, and Oklahoma as well.

4. Simms (through his protagonist) contrasts youthful "gratification of . . . passions and desires" with mature "reflection, which is the result of training and habit" (60).

5. E. A. Duyckinck, *Literary World* 5 (August 25, 1849): 159.

APPENDICES

Historical Background

It is as a Border novel that *Helen Halsey* should be read and studied—and the historical sketches accompanying *Richard Hurdis* and *Border Beagles* are particularly relevant for this volume as well. The gang of outlaws led by Bud Halsey is not as directly based on the crime syndicate of John A. Murrell as was the Mystic Brotherhood of the earlier Border Romances, but the concept of a broad-based organization supported by corrupt politicians and public officials is the same. As in the cases of the other outlaw bands, both in real life and in fiction, the rampage of terror and lawlessness which occurred under the reign of Bud Halsey was ended by an eruption of public outrage and the execution of "frontier" justice. In the words of Simms in the conclusion to *Helen Halsey,*

> the ultimate extinction of Indian title to the lands, was an event, of itself, to strike a fatal blow at the security of the 'government-against-law' in Conelachita. How the people, furious in consequence of the most frequent and audacious murders, to say nothing of robberies, rushed *en masse* into the swamp-fastnesses, and, with shot, and sabre-strike, and halter, put an end to the dynasty of the outlaw, in that quarter. [125]

One difference between *Halsey* and all the other Border Romances needs some explanation, however: whereas *Guy Rivers* is clearly set in Georgia, *Richard Hurdis* in Alabama, *Border Beagles* in Mississippi, and *Beauchampe* in Kentucky—to mention only those which precede 1845— Simms seems to wish to avoid giving *Helen Halsey* an identifiable setting. Where is the "Swamp State of Conelachita"? And what is the "Swamp State of Conelachita"? On first reading, one probably assumes that Conelachita is the name Simms has given Louisiana: *Helen Halsey* is dedicated to "Randell Hunt, Esq. of Louisiana," a suggestion that the book is appropriate for Louisiana; Louisiana is also the next state in line in the westward progression through Georgia, Alabama, and Mississippi (with Kentucky somewhere aside). But the word *Louisiana* appears nowhere in *Helen Halsey*—somewhat surprising in the light of Simms's specificity in the very subtitles of the other novels ("A Tale of Georgia," "A Tale of Alabama," etc.). It seems that Simms intended "Conelachita" as the name of the outlaws' extensive swamp kingdom—not as the fictional name for a political state in the U.S.—in which case the "Swamp State of Conelachita" may have existed within or over the borders of several Gulf Coast states (most likely, Louisiana and Mississippi), not merely one. Early in his search for a publisher Simms referred to what became *Helen Halsey* as "a Tale of Mississippi," adding confusion to the clouded issue—as does the fact that Mississippi (as well as Alabama and Tennessee—and New Orleans, but not Louisiana) is referred to by name in the published version.[1] The most logical conclusion seems to be that Simms early thought of his novelette as set in Mississippi, but perhaps changed his mind upon deciding to dedicate the book to his friend from Louisiana, Randell Hunt. Simms's eventual resolution apparently was to leave the "Swamp State of Conelachita" intentionally ambiguous—it was simply a swamp setting in one or more of the coastal states bordering the Gulf and the Mississippi River. That the setting is appropriate to the mode of action and the description of landscape is the only matter of relevance.

Note

1. The fact that the Reverend Mr. Mowbray is identified with New Orleans (76) perhaps hints that Conelachita is located in Louisiana; but the protagonist's supposition, ". . . should the government of the United States, or Mississippi, ever find it necessary to send a sufficient force into our swamp retreat" (61), implies that Mississippi serves as the location of the events depicted.

References

Clark, Thomas D., and John D. W. Guice. *Frontiers in Conflict: The Old Southwest, 1795–1830*. Albuquerque: University of New Mexico Press, 1989.

Gayarré, Charles Étienne Arthur. *History of Louisiana: The American Domination*. New York: William J. Widdleton, 1866.

McLemore, Richard Aubrey, ed. *A History of Mississippi*. Vol. 1. Jackson: University and College Press of Mississippi, 1973.

Penick, James Lal, Jr. *The Great Western Land Pirate: John A. Murrell in Legend and History*. Columbia: University of Missouri Press, 1981.

Explanatory Notes

CHAPTER THREE

p. 11, line 31 *Honi soit qui mal y pense:* cursed be he who thinks evil of it.

p. 13, line 30 discussed: consumed enthusiastically.

CHAPTER FOUR

p. 17, line 21 swamps of Choctawhatchie: unidentified, probably fictitious.

CHAPTER SIX

p. 25, line 18 Alsatia: cant name given to the Whitefriars district in London, because of the lawless characters and libertines who sought privileges of sanctuary at the monastery.

p. 26, line 22–23 Woodstock was a fool to the swamp city of Conelachita!: in Sir Walter Scott's *Woodstock* (1826), Woodstock was the old lodge and park used as a place of concealment for the fugitive Charles II.

p. 27, line 5 my own noble river, the Alabama: river flowing in a southwesterly direction from central Alabama to Mobile.

p. 29, line 9–10 Franklin County, West Tennessee: Franklin County is in southeast central Tennessee, not west Tennessee.

CHAPTER SIXTEEN

p. 69, line 3 Boanerges: surname given by Jesus to James and John; a vociferous preacher.

CHAPTER SEVENTEEN

p. 80, line 21 Long Parliament: the Parliament which assembled in November 1640 was expelled by Cromwell in 1653, reconvened in 1659, and was dissolved in 1660.

p. 80, line 23 Waller: Edmund Waller (1607–87), "smooth" and "sweet" English poet.

p. 80, line 24 Rochester: John Wilmot, Second Earl of Rochester (1647–80), rakish English cavalier poet.

p. 82, line 17 Coventry: English city famous for its plays (the implication is that Mowbray was playacting).

CHAPTER EIGHTEEN

p. 84, line 23 Quoits: a game in which the players pitch flat iron rings, called *quoits,* at a pin.

CHAPTER NINETEEN

p. 88, line 26 Cedar Island: in Mississippi, a Cedar Island is found in Hancock County, just southeast of Ansley (Saint Joe Pass topographic map, 1994).*

p. 88, line 27 Buffalo Bend: unidentified, probably fictitious.

p. 89, line 11 Fawn's Point: unidentified, probably fictitious.

CHAPTER TWENTY

p. 92, line 24–25 cry of a dozen beagles: in *Border Beagles* the Mystic Brotherhood used imitations of the bay of beagles to send signals; the same device is apparently also used by Bud Halsey's gang.

CHAPTER TWENTY-THREE

p. 103, line 15 Baker's Landing: in Louisiana; a Baker's Landing is listed in *GNIS: Geographic Names Information System, Digital Gazetter* (U.S. Geological survey, 1996). Baker's Landing is located in Quachita County, just north of Monroe on the Quachita River.*

CHAPTER TWENTY-FOUR

p. 107, line 4 *soi distant:* so-called.

p. 108, line 37 Raccoon crossing: unidentified, probably fictitious.

---

* I am indebted to Janet B. Dixon, map librarian, University of Arkansas, for locating Cedar Island and Baker's Landing.

Textual Notes

Since it is highly unlikely that Simms, in the year before his death, saw through the press the serial republication of *Helen Halsey* (under the title "The Island Bride") in *New York Fireside Companion* for February 24, March 9, March 16, March 23, March 30, April 6, and April 14, 1869, I have chosen to ignore textually this seven-installment periodical republication and have used as copy-text for the Arkansas Edition the first (and only) book publication: *Helen Halsey: or, The Swamp State of Conelachita. A Tale of the Borders.* By W. Gilmore Simms, Author of "Richard Hurdis," "The Yemassee," "The Kinsmen," &c. New-York: Burgess, Stringer & Co., 1845. Dedication to Randell Hunt, Esq., of Louisiana.

In the Burgess, Stringer edition, the chapter numbers appear as Roman numerals and periods follow the chapter titles. Throughout the Arkansas Edition, chapter titles are spelled out and the periods following the chapter titles are omitted.

EMENDATIONS

Listed below to the left of the brackets are accidentals as they appear in the 1845 Burgess, Stringer edition of *Helen Halsey;* to the right of the brackets are emendations by the editor for the Arkansas Edition. The citation in the left-hand margin is to the page and line in the Arkansas Edition on which the emendation occurs. Simms's nineteenth-century style of orthography and punctuation has not been emended, except for what are judged to be printer's errors.

Dedication	or] of
3.15	cold] could
9.18	as the] as to the
9.38	startlight] starlight
12.35	Not] "Not
13.33	humoredly.] humoredly:
21.14	ocurring] occurring
25.17	. some] . Some
30.17	mor ethan] more than
37.11	Ellen] Helen
53.22	please, But] please, but
53.28	upon be] be upon
77.13	heaven!"] heaven!
79.03	undertaken] undertaken.
84.05	became] become

86.13	me?] me.
87.20	think!] think!"
89.03	an] and
104.24	recknoing] reckoning

Select Bibliography

LETTERS

The Letters of William Gilmore Simms. Ed. Mary C. Simms Oliphant, Alfred
    Taylor Odell, and T. C. Duncan Eaves. 5 vols. Columbia: University of
    South Carolina Press, 1952–1956. (Cited in Introduction and Afterword
    as L, followed by volume and page number.)
The Letters of William Gilmore Simms. Ed. Mary C. Simms Oliphant and T. C.
    Duncan Eaves. Supplement, Vol. VI. Columbia: University of South
    Carolina Press, 1982.

MODERN COLLECTIONS

Selected Poems of William Gilmore Simms. Ed. James Everett Kibler Jr. Athens:
    University of Georgia Press, 1990.
Stories and Tales. Ed. John Caldwell Guilds. (Vol. 5 of *The Writings of William
    Gilmore Simms: Centennial Edition*). Columbia: University of South
    Carolina Press, 1974.
Tales of the South by William Gilmore Simms. Ed. Mary Ann Wimsatt.
    Columbia: University of South Carolina Press, 1996.

BIOGRAPHY

Guilds, John Caldwell. *Simms: A Literary Life.* Fayetteville: University of
    Arkansas Press, 1992.
Trent, William P. *William Gilmore Simms.* (American Men of Letters Series).
    Boston: Houghton Mifflin, 1892.

GENERAL CRITICISM AND STUDIES

Davidson, Donald. "Introduction." In *The Letters of William Gilmore Simms,*
    Vol. I. Columbia: University of South Carolina Press, 1952. [see xxxi–clii;
    early, highly appreciative estimate of Simms's fiction]
Faust, Drew Gilpin. *A Sacred Circle: The Dilemma of the Intellectual in the Old
    South, 1840–1860.* Baltimore: Johns Hopkins University Press, 1977.
    [deals extensively and perceptively with Simms as Southern intellectual]
Gray, Richard. *Writing the South: Ideas of an American Region.* Cambridge:
    Cambridge University Press, 1986. [see "To Speak of Arcadia: William
    Gilmore Simms and Some Plantation Novelists," 45–62]
Guilds, John Caldwell, ed. *"Long Years of Neglect": The Work and Reputation of
    William Gilmore Simms.* Fayetteville: University of Arkansas Press, 1988.
    [evaluative essays by Guilds, James B. Meriwether, Anne M. Blythe, Linda

E. McDaniel, Nicholas G. Meriwether, James E. Kibler Jr., David Moltke-
Hansen, Mary Ann Wimsatt, Rayburn S. Moore, Miriam J. Shillingsburg,
John McCardell, and Louis D. Rubin Jr.]

———— and Caroline Collins, ed. *William Gilmore Simms and the American
Frontier.* Athens: University of Georgia Press, 1997. [collection of essays
on different aspects of Simms's extensive treatment of the frontier]

Hubbell, Jay B. *The South in American Literature, 1607–1900.* [Durham]: Duke
University Press, 1954. [chapter on Simms, 572–602; still one of the best
short essays on the author]

Kolodny, Annette. *The Lay of the Land: Metaphors as Experience and History in
American Life and Letters.* Chapel Hill: University of North Carolina
Press, 1975. [see 115–32; perceptive analysis of Simms's depiction of
landscape]

Kreyling, Michael. *Figures of the Hero in Southern Narrative.* Baton Rouge:
Louisiana State University Press, 1987. [see "William Gilmore Simms:
Writer and Hero," 30–51]

McHaney, Thomas L. "William Gilmore Simms." In *The Chief Glory of Every
People: Essays on Classic American Writers.* Ed. Matthew J. Bruccoli,
173–90. Carbondale: Southern Illinois University Press, 1973. [notable
for its recognition of the significance of Border novels]

Parrington, Vernon L. *The Romantic Revolution in America, 1800–1860.* New
York: Harcourt, Brace, 1927. Vol. II of *Main Currents in American
Thought.* 3 vols. 1927–1930. [chapter on Simms, 125–36; an important
early assessment of his achievements]

Ridgely, J. V. *William Gilmore Simms.* (Twayne's United States Authors Series).
New York: Twayne, 1962.

Rubin, Louis D., Jr. *The Edge of the Swamp: A Study in the Literature and Society
of the Old South.* Baton Rouge: Louisiana State University Press, 1989.
[see "The Dream of the Plantation: Simms, Hammond, Charleston,"
54–102; and "The Romance of the Frontier: Simms, Cooper, and the
Wilderness," 103–26]

Shillingsburg, Miriam J. "The Senior Simmses—Mississippi Unshrouded."
University of Mississippi Studies in English, n.s. 2 (1992): 250–55.
[genealogical and historical information about Simms's father and uncle
in Mississippi]

Thomas, J. Wesley. "William Gilmore Simms' 'Helen Halsey' as the Source for
Friedrich Gerstäcker's 'Germelshausen.'" *Monatshefte* 45 (1853): 141–44.
[concludes that Gerstäcker, translator of *The Wigwam and the Cabin* and
probably other works by Simms, made conscious use of *Helen Halsey* in
plotting his own novel]

Wakelyn, Jon L. *The Politics of a Literary Man: William Gilmore Simms.* Westport, Conn.: Greenwood, 1973.

Wimsatt, Mary Ann. *The Major Fiction of William Gilmore Simms: Cultural Traditions and Literary Form.* Baton Rouge: Louisiana State University Press, 1989. [valuable study focusing on the Revolutionary Romances and Simms's use of humor throughout his fiction]

REFERENCE WORK

Butterworth, Keen and James E. Kibler Jr. *William Gilmore Simms: A Reference Guide.* Boston: G. K. Hall, 1980. [contemporary notices of *Helen Halsey* are very briefly summarized, 57, 59]

DATE DUE

WITHDRAWN

HIGHSMITH #45230

Printed
in USA